"Help!"

The door flew open. Adam was standing on the other side of it.

"Adam, do you think you could help me get out of this water bed?"

"Oh, sure." Adam stumbled toward Leah and leaned forward to rip the sheet off her body.

Leah gasped, startled by the speed and aggression of his movement. Adam let his gaze r___ ver the beautiful woman stretched ____

"You're very pre___ straighten___

As he did s_____ __. He threw his ar_____ nimself to keep them bo___

"Adam, you c___ go now," she said clearly.

"In a minute," he murmured.

Leah rather enjoyed his cozy embrace. He smelled musky from sleep, and his body felt strong and slim and heavy. He seemed to be getting heavier by the second, actually.

"Adam? Adam?"

Leah pinched him sharply. "You're falling back asleep," she said, feeling perversely insulted.

Dear Reader:

Spring is in the air! Birds are singing, flowers are blooming and thoughts are turning to love. Since springtime is such a romantic time, I'm happy to say that April's Silhouette Desires are the very essence of romance.

Now we didn't exactly plan it this way, but three of our books this month are connecting stories. *The Hidden Pearl* by Celeste Hamilton is part of **Aunt Eugenia's Treasures**. *Ladies' Man* by Raye Morgan ties into *Husband for Hire* (#434). And our *Man of the Month*, Garret Cagan in Ann Major's *Scandal's Child* ties into her successful **Children of Destiny** series.

I know many of you love connecting stories, but if you haven't read the "prequels" and spin-offs, please remember that each and every Silhouette Desire is a wonderful love story in its own right.

And don't miss our other April books: *King of the Mountain* by Joyce Thies, *Guilty Secrets* by Laura Leone and *Sunshine* by Jo Ann Algermissen!

Before I go, I have to say that I'd love to know what you think about our new covers. Please write in and let me know. I'm always curious about what the readers think—and I also believe that your thoughts are important.

Until next month,

Lucia Macro
Senior Editor

LAURA LEONE

GUILTY SECRETS

SILHOUETTE *Desire*

Published by Silhouette Books New York
America's Publisher of Contemporary Romance

Books by Laura Leone

Silhouette Desire

One Sultry Summer #478
A Wilder Name #507
Ulterior Motives #531
Guilty Secrets #560

LAURA LEONE

grew up in the Midwest and has been on the move, traveling throughout the world, since she was nineteen. Back in the United States for the time being, Laura teaches French, Italian and English to adults and "drifts a lot."

With thanks to Ivy Mitchell,
a scholar and a lady,
and to certain members of my family,
human and otherwise.

One

***

Adam Jordan stared at the dense, heavy, stagnant, labored prose on the page in front of him and sighed. He was beginning to think it would take a sorcerer to make Verbena's work readable.

> *Less contiguous, though certainly easily rendered moreso by an equally prohibitive social context laboring under misapprehensions brought about by almost unceasing military conflict overwhelming those normally productive agricultural counties that were, in previous centuries, more intellectually progressive, if not more...*

"Good grief," he muttered. If he, Verbena's collaborator, couldn't decipher her meaning, how on earth did she expect their readers to be able to? They had already talked about this several times, but it was clear he would have to bring up the subject again.

Adam glanced out the window of the bedroom he had been staying in for the past two weeks. Verbena's property extended back for five acres, most of it obscured by trees. He could see her standing just a few yards away from the back porch, her shoulders straight and strong despite her age, her white hair and yellow jumpsuit standing out against the lush green summer lawn.

He considered going straight down to talk to her about her incomprehensible prose, hoping to stop her before she wrote again, but decided against it. Despite nearly forty years in the academic world, she was still rather sensitive to criticism, and he didn't have the heart to see those brown eyes look hurt today.

Especially not today. Today Professor Verbena Mc-Cargar was as happy as a frisky puppy. Her son and her niece were both coming home for the summer, and they were due sometime before dinner.

Although Adam had known Verbena on and off for years, he knew very little about her family. Since she used her maiden name and had never mentioned a husband, Adam supposed her son, Mordred, was illegitimate. Since she had never volunteered the information, he didn't ask; it was none of his business.

He knew only a little more about Verbena's niece, Leah. Verbena had bragged about the girl's beauty and academic brilliance, explaining that Leah's parents had been killed when she was young. As the nearest living relation, Verbena had taken responsibility for raising Leah thereafter.

Verbena had accompanied this brief explanation with the usual mandatory photos: Leah as a thin, pale child with wide, frightened dark eyes, shortly after coming to live with Verbena; Mordred, looked cocky and cool with his high-school prom date; Leah, still with dark, serious eyes, proudly holding up her high-school diploma.

Both kids were now adults in their late twenties, and neither had been able to visit Verbena for nearly two years.

Adam saw Verbena tilt her head and stand alertly as if she had heard a car pulling up. After a moment she shook her head ruefully. No, he decided, he definitely wouldn't bother her with business this afternoon. He would plow through this mess by himself today.

"Adam?" Verbena called.

"Yeah?" he shouted down through the screened window.

"Keep your ears pricked for a while, will you? I'm going to go feed the raccoons down by the stream."

"Okay," he replied. He smiled to himself as he turned back to his typewriter. Verbena probably fed half the wildlife around the Finger Lakes. Raccoons, possums, deer, squirrels, birds—if it was hungry, it could come to Verbena's house for chow.

"All right, let's see what we can do with this." He spoke to himself, as he often did when working. He stretched, closed his eyes for a moment and then tackled the job with his customary absorption, blocking out everything else and becoming immersed in his thoughts.

Within half an hour, he was typing quickly, tossing aside Verbena's pages of notes one by one as he rewrote them in a readable, conversational style.

"Good, good, good... Not too bad... The fifteenth century..."

The doorbell rang. The house erupted with noise as half a dozen pets burst into a chorus of welcome and made a beeline for the front door.

"Arrgh," Adam groaned, running a hand through his dark blond hair. They had been so busy with research lately, this was the first chance he'd had to actually work on the book in several days.

"Just when it was going well, too," he muttered, switching off his electric typewriter. He glanced one last time at the page he was working on, then shrugged. "I guess the Renaissance will just have to wait a little longer."

Halfway down the stairs he was struck by a new idea, one that would neatly tie up the various threads of thought in their book's introduction. He frowned briefly, wondering if Verbena would like it. She might consider it too general, too commercial. He would have to broach the idea carefully. If only she could unlearn the staid, uninspired, dusty rules she had lived by her entire professional life.

The doorbell rang again. Macbeth, a sable collie, barked impatiently, eager to greet the newcomer. Dismissing his problem for the moment, Adam descended the rest of the steps and crossed the big, high-ceilinged entrance hallway to open the door and greet Verbena's son and niece.

Leah McCargar stood alone on the wide front porch of her Aunt Verbena's big, welcoming old house. She smiled as she heard eager barking and scratching on the other side of the door. Her aunt's ever-growing menagerie was on hand to welcome her home.

The door opened at last, and Leah's greeting died on her lips.

"Hi, Leah," said a man who looked golden from head to foot, except for his bright blue eyes. "Where's Mordred?"

Before Leah had time to respond to the total stranger who evidently recognized her, she was lovingly assaulted by Macbeth, two Siamese cats she remembered as Tristram and Isolde, and two other dogs she didn't recognize.

"Here, I'll take your suitcase," shouted the man above the uproar. "You'd better come inside before King John escapes."

"Who's King John? Who are *you*?" Leah asked in confusion. He appeared quite at home as he took her case from her, picked up a few stray dog toys and guided her past three furry bodies, all lying belly-up and whining for attention.

"I'm Adam," he said, as if that explained everything.

"What are you—"

"Oh, no! There goes the ferret!" He dropped her suitcase with a thud and shot out the door with the speed of an Olympic athlete.

Leah stared after him. This was not quite the homecoming she had expected. Whoever he was, Adam was certainly an appealing sight: tall, slim and muscular, slightly disheveled, with rumpled golden hair and clear blue eyes. However, after the long trip from California, she would have preferred to meet someone familiar at the door of the house she had grown up in.

Leah heard the back door slam. "Hello?" she called.

Her aunt's voice trilled through the house. "Leah! Leah, dear, is that you?"

"In here, Auntie!" Leah called, her way blocked by three friendly, intensely curious dogs.

A moment later Verbena McCargar rushed into the entrance hall. Small and slightly plump, with shining white hair and lively brown eyes, she seized Leah with her seemingly frail arms and enveloped her in a crushing embrace.

"Oh, Leah!" she cried. "It's so good to see you! You should have let me come to the airport to get you!"

"After last time, I thought it would be wiser to take a taxi," Leah said dryly. Upon her arrival for her past visit two years ago, her aunt had been so absorbed in sharing all the latest news that she had driven straight off the road. Fortunately, no one was hurt, but a number of shopkeepers were extremely inconvenienced for several days.

"Where's Mordred?" Verbena asked.

Leah's smile faded. She braced herself for the disappointment she knew she would see in her aunt's eyes. "He called me from L.A. this morning, Auntie, just before I left Palo Alto, to say he's been delayed."

"Delayed?" Verbena's eyes misted slightly with dismay. "When will he be here?"

"Very soon, Auntie, he promised," Leah assured her. Actually Mordred had promised no such thing. He had called Leah in a state of panic to say he couldn't meet her as planned at LaGuardia for the connecting flight to Ithaca. He had offered no explanation, begged her to break it to

Verbena herself and promised to be in touch as soon as it was "safe."

Leah was worried by both the tone and content of that brief conversation, but Mordred had hung up before she could press him for details. She had called him back immediately, but there was no answer at his apartment. So she would wait to hear from him again. In the meantime, she would keep her aunt from worrying about him.

"You know how busy he is," Leah reminded Verbena.

"Yes, yes, of course." Verbena made a brave little attempt to shrug off her obvious disappointment. Then she smiled and embraced Leah again. "At least I have you here. That should be enough of a treat for me after all this time."

"I'm sorry it's been so long, Auntie. I just—"

"I know. I know what life is like for you ambitious graduate students. You must be famished, dear! We've prepared a lovely dinner—" Verbena abruptly stopped speaking and looked around. "But where's Adam?"

"He let me in, then said something about a ferret and dashed out the door." Leah raised her dark brows inquisitively.

"Oh, that's King John."

"So I gathered. What on earth is a ferret doing—"

"Adorable, isn't he? I bought him from the pet shop last fall, and he was terribly sweet and content until just recently. He's taken to running out the front door every time he gets the chance. Of course, he can go out the back door anytime he wants, since the backyard is all fenced in, but the front door, being forbidden, seems to hold a particular challenge—"

"Auntie," Leah interrupted. "Who is that man?"

"That's Adam, dear. Do you want to wash up before—"

"What's he doing here? Does he do yard work or something?"

"Hardly," said a deep masculine voice behind her. "But I'm not above helping, if suitably bribed." Leah turned to see Adam cradling a long, slinky mammal in one arm as he closed the front door. "Here's your ferret, Verbena. I'm really getting into shape chasing him around the country-side a dozen times a week."

"Come here, King John," crooned Verbena, taking him from Adam. The ferret curled up against Verbena and glanced malevolently at Adam.

"I'm glad to meet you at last, Leah," Adam said. "I've heard so much about you, all of it impossibly good."

"Oh," Leah said, still somewhat bewildered. She took his proffered hand, noting how hard and strong it was, with long, slim fingers. "I'm afraid I've heard nothing about you," she admitted, glancing at Verbena.

"Didn't I tell you about Adam when you called, dear?" said Verbena with an absent frown. "How remiss of me. Well, let me make amends now. Adam is a colleague who's staying here while we work."

"Colleague?" Leah repeated in astonishment. "Surely you're not ... I mean ..."

"We're collaborating on a book," Adam supplied.

"I *did* mention I would be working with a colleague on a book all summer, didn't I, dear?"

"Yes, you did mention that. I just didn't realize..." Leah let the sentence trail off rather awkwardly. She couldn't very well say that Adam looked more like an athlete or an actor than a medieval historian. Certainly none of *her* history professors had ever looked like him.

"I slaved half the day making a wonderful dinner, so why don't we sit down to enjoy it," Adam suggested.

"That sounds wonderful. I'm famished," said Leah, relieved to know she wouldn't be immediately subjected to Verbena's cooking.

Since this was Leah's welcome-home dinner, they ate in the formal dining room. Verbena's home, set in the countryside outside of Ithaca, New York, was more than a century old. It boasted three floors of large rooms, plus a cellar and an attic. The rooms were graced by high ceilings, tall windows, smooth oak floors and Verbena's own eclectic style of decorating.

Although a house that size might seem too large to most people, Verbena needed nearly that much wall space just to hold all of her books. Leah's aunt was one of the most renowned medievalists in the country and owned one of the largest private collections of books in her field.

Verbena briefly explained to Adam that Mordred had been forced to postpone his visit for undisclosed reasons. Adam thought it inconsiderate of Mordred to disappoint his doting mother after such a long time, but he simply voiced a polite comment and smiled flirtatiously at Leah as they all sat down to dinner.

Adam served pasta primavera, fresh salad and thick, crusty bread. He grinned at Leah's expression of delight and guessed that she had steeled herself for a summer of Verbena's dreadful cooking. After only a few days in the house he had decided to take over the cooking as a matter of self-preservation.

He had to admit to himself that Leah had grown up to be as lovely as her aunt had said. He had assumed till now that Verbena was describing her with the generosity of a loving relative, but as Leah smiled fondly at her aunt and laughed over stories about King John and the Siamese cats, he agreed with Verbena's assessment that she was someone special.

He knew from his previous conversation with Verbena that Leah was twenty-seven years old. Now he saw that her skin was pale and smooth, emphasizing the richly deep brown color of her eyes and of her thick, shoulder-length hair. She was slightly taller than average, and though slim, she possessed subtly ripe curves in all the right places. She was dressed in a simple cotton dress and wore a minimum of makeup. The simplicity definitely suited her, he decided.

At the moment she was devouring his cooking with the enthusiasm all students showed for free food.

"Verbena tells me you're entering the last year of your Ph.D. work, Leah," he said.

"Yes. Medieval history, of course," she replied, glancing at Verbena.

"Is your thesis all that you have left to do?" Adam asked.

"Not quite," Leah admitted. "There's a statistics course I've been putting off for quite some time. I'll have to take it in the fall."

Adam grimaced. "I remember that. In fact, Verbena was my teacher."

Leah looked surprised. "You were one of her students?"

"Just for my M.A. I took my stats courses then just to get them over with. And let me tell you, Verbena's class was sheer hell."

"Oh, come now," Verbena protested.

"This sweet, white-haired lady is a veritable dragon with her master's students, always trying to sort out the chaff from the wheat," Adam said teasingly. "I was terrified of her my whole first year."

"Terrified?" Verbena exclaimed in indignation. "Leah, dear, I couldn't get *rid* of the boy. It was always, 'Professor McCargar, have you got a few minutes?', 'Professor McCargar, can you read my article and tell me what you think?', 'Professor McCargar, will you marry me?'"

Leah choked on her pasta. "He actually asked you to marry him?"

"Of course. My students always fall in love with me," Verbena said smugly.

Adam grinned at Verbena but didn't deny it. Leah looked back and forth between the two of them and felt a faint twinge of suspicion. Adam appeared to be in his mid-thirties, a whole generation younger than Verbena's usual colleagues. Physically he was a far cry from the stereotypically stooped, jaundiced, myopic scholar. Even on the periphery of his dazzling smile, she could feel the devastating force of his charm. She wondered what kind of credentials he had. She wondered if he had ever written a book before, or even any noteworthy articles. She wondered what, besides his beach-boy looks and personal charm, made him worthy of a partnership with her estimable aunt.

"So tell me more about this book you two are working on," she insisted.

"We're calling it *A Viable Alternative*," Verbena said enthusiastically.

"I still say we need a catchier title," Adam interrupted.

"I'd been wanting to do this book for a while, and when I approached Adam—"

"You approached Adam?" Leah interrupted in surprise.

"Yes."

"Where did you get your Ph.D., Adam?" Leah asked. Certainly he had a doctorate. Her aunt would never work with an unqualified collaborator.

Leah's eyes were unfathomable, but Adam had the feeling her question was prompted by more than polite interest. There was a brief, uncomfortable pause before Verbena said, "Barrington, wasn't it, Adam?"

"Barrington University? That's an excellent program. A friend of mine is starting there in the fall." Leah looked at Adam assessingly.

"Really?" Adam's voice was dry and noncommittal.

"Yes. How long were you there?"

"Three years." The questions were harmless and typical, and Leah asked them in a smooth, conversational tone, but he had no doubt that she was sizing him up. Adam didn't like being sized up after a few minutes' acquaintance, and he particularly didn't like to have his character judged on the basis of his academic accomplishments.

"Do you teach somewhere?" Leah prodded, noticing that the loquacious golden boy had suddenly run out of patter.

"No." Before Leah could fill the silence with more questions he didn't feel like answering during a pleasant family dinner, Adam grinned at her, pushed back his chair and said, "Why don't you let Verbena tell you about our frankly excellent book while I go into the kitchen and bring out my frankly excellent dessert."

"He certainly doesn't lack self-confidence, does he?" Leah said blandly as she watched him disappear through the swinging wooden door.

Verbena smiled broadly, her dark eyes shining with fondness. "No, he doesn't. But he *was* one of my best students. And he is a very good writer." Verbena looked down at her hands. "After my last book, I decided I needed a fresh approach to my work."

"Oh, Auntie, you're not still letting that bother you, are you?" said Leah sympathetically.

Verbena shrugged. Her last book, *Ecclesiastical Influence on Domestic Life under the Early Plantagenet Kings* had been received with dignified approbation in scholarly circles. Critics and columnists, however, had generally lambasted the tome, saying Verbena's exhaustive research had been wasted on prose that was dull, heavy, repetitious and so indecipherable as to be unreadable. Leah had spent many hours in long-distance telephone conversations comforting Verbena, who was distraught over the vindictive criticism.

Avoiding Leah's eyes, Verbena poured more wine into the three goblets on the table. "So you decided to collaborate with young blood?" Leah said, trying to force enthusiasm into her voice.

"Yes, exactly," Verbena said, brightening a little.

"I'm sure Adam is glad for the opportunity. No doubt it will give his own work added credibility." A collaboration with Verbena McCargar, even in light of her recent failure, would be a feather in the cap of any young historian.

"Yes, it will." Verbena frowned briefly. "When I said that to him, he told me I was an insufferable snob."

Leah's jaw dropped in disbelief. "Then why on earth did you still want to collaborate with him?"

"Oh, for a number of reasons. I've always preferred teaching and researching to writing, you know that. He loves to write, which leaves me more time to do research. He's done some work on the topic before. He's very bright and full of unusual ideas, so I was sure our association would be stimulating. And,'' she added, raising her voice as Adam entered the room, "I am rather fond of him, despite his numerous quirks and flaws.''

"What quirks? What flaws?'' Adam demanded as he placed a bowl full of extremely fattening food in front of Leah.

Leah dug into her dessert and closed her eyes in ecstasy as fresh berries, cream, angel food cake and kirsch permeated her tastebuds. "Oh, this is heaven!''

"Evidently my cooking makes up for my character flaws in your niece's eyes,'' Adam told Verbena.

"Ah, we'll see about that,'' said Verbena. "Leah is very protective of her loved ones. You'll have to do more than whip up a few fancy dishes to win her faith.''

"Is that a fact?'' Adam's eyes rested curiously on Leah.

Leah shrugged noncommittally and continued devouring her dessert. Out of the corner of her eye, she saw something pass by the table. She turned to look at it more clearly. After a moment of stunned disbelief, she let out a yelp, dropped her spoon and drew both long legs up to the seat of her chair.

"Leah, dear, what's wrong?'' exclaimed Verbena.

"What is *that*?''

Adam followed the direction of Leah's startled brown gaze.

"Oh, that,'' he said wearily as a timid reptile crept toward the table. "That's the Questing Beast.''

"It looks like an iguana,'' Leah said, peering cautiously over the table at its hideous face.

"He *is* an iguana, dear,'' Verbena interjected. "I saw him—''

"At the pet shop,'' Leah said resignedly.

"And she couldn't resist him,'' Adam added.

"He looked so lonesome,'' Leah went on.

"And she was afraid of what would happen to him if no one bought him," Adam finished.

"Well...yes," said Verbena, somewhat perplexed. "How did you know?"

Adam and Leah looked at each other. Adam rolled his eyes.

"He's terribly shy," Verbena explained, "but very affectionate once he gets to know you."

"Affectionate?" Leah said disbelievingly. "*Affectionate?* You mean he—he—" She looked pleadingly at Adam, who mercilessly supplied the details.

"Curls up with you while you're watching TV. Watches you brush your teeth at night. Sleeps near you while you're reading or writing. Loves to—"

"Stop! Please, stop," she interrupted him. "I don't think I want to hear any more."

"You *have* met the mynah bird, haven't you?" Adam asked conversationally.

"Archimedes? The one that lives in the first-floor study? Yes, he's been here for years. He's at least tolerable. But an iguana? Auntie, didn't you learn your lesson after Kubla Khan?"

"But the Questing Beast is very sweet and placid, Leah. It's not the same situation at all," Verbena protested. "Besides, he doesn't have Kubla Khan's nasty dietary habits."

"Wait a minute," Adam interrupted, his interest perking. "Who is Kubla Khan?"

Leah gestured to her aunt, offering her the opportunity to explain.

"I gave Kubla Khan to my son, Mordred, for his sixteenth birthday. He was a very difficult reptile. That's really all there is to tell. Now, why don't we talk about—"

"Kubla Khan," Leah said sternly, "was a Burmese python with the temper of a wounded tiger."

"He could be a little testy at times," Verbena admitted sheepishly.

"My cousin Mordred detests animals, particularly reptiles, and certainly didn't want him."

"How that boy could hate animals after growing up in this house is beyond me," said Verbena, shaking her head sadly.

"Inconceivable," said Adam dryly as Tristram and Isolde, the two Siamese cats, tore across the table, knocking down a glass of wine and puncturing the tablecloth.

"The snake was four feet long when Auntie bought him. By the following summer, he was seventeen feet long," Leah said.

Adam's blue eyes widened as he looked at Leah with a mixture of horror and amusement. "A seventeen-foot-long Burmese python as a house pet?"

"My aunt has no doubt already told you how she feels about caging animals—"

"Cruel! Inhumane! Savage! How would *you* like to spend the rest of your life in a little glass or wire cubicle?" Verbena cried, ready to lecture on a favorite topic.

"Obviously a foul-tempered snake that size couldn't be left to roam around the house freely. So Verbena gave him a whole bedroom of his own to live in."

"He had a bedroom of his own?" Adam mused. Then he quickly demanded, "Which one?"

"Don't worry, dear, not yours," Verbena said. "It was on the third floor."

"Kubla Khan naturally had to be fed live food. Since Verbena couldn't stand to participate in sending innocent little creatures to their deaths in his room, she made Mordred do it."

"I *paid* him to do it," Verbena corrected. "He wouldn't do it for free."

"Smart kid," murmured Adam.

"Things just got out of hand somehow," said Verbena. "Kubla Khan was very strong and devious, and he broke out of his room twice that summer. The town decided we were a public menace, and none of my colleagues would come here to visit. One day the snake attacked Mordred, and after that there wasn't enough money in all the world to induce Mordred to keep taking care of him."

"So what finally happened?" Adam asked.

"Leah took charge, of course."

"You wrestled the snake and won?" Adam's eyes roved over their slender, sloe-eyed companion.

"I called a zoo and told them Verbena would make a generous donation if they'd take the snake off her hands."

"Very sensible."

"I suppose it was for the best," Verbena said sadly.

"And you still haven't learned your lesson," Leah said in exasperation. "How big will the Questing Beast get?"

"He's grown four inches in the two weeks I've been here," Adam offered.

"Auntie?"

"He's supposed to stop growing when he's about six feet long, I think."

"Six feet! And where are you going to keep a reptile that size once the weather gets cold?" Leah demanded.

Verbena shrugged. "I haven't quite worked that out yet."

Adam leaned back in his chair, watching the two of them. This was clearly another problem Leah intended to take care of. It was probably just as well. He had already realized that someone had to consider the impracticality of keeping an iguana as a house pet, but he was in no position to interfere with Verbena's domestic life. Evidently Leah knew how to deal with her.

Clearly intending to change the subject, Verbena rose from her chair and said, "After that lovely meal, wouldn't everyone like a lovely cup of coffee? I'll be back in just a moment."

After she left the room Adam smiled at Leah. "I've often wondered why Verbena's son visits her so infrequently. I'm beginning to understand."

Leah shrugged in mild agreement. "I guess Mordred has had his reasons for staying away. He had a pretty mind-bending youth."

"Where does he live now?"

"In Los Angeles. He figured it was the farthest he could get from Verbena and still remain in the continental U.S."

Adam laughed. "So if he's in L.A. and you're in Palo Alto, do you stay in touch?"

"Oh, yes. Mordred and I are the same age, and we've always been very close."

There was a slight pause before Adam said, "Verbena was so pleased to hear that both of you would be visiting this summer."

"Yes..." Leah said hesitantly.

Adam studied her shrewdly. "You talked him into it, didn't you?"

She nodded. She frowned, thinking. Aside from the fact that Verbena was hurt that Mordred didn't visit her more often, Leah had felt it would be good for him to get out of L.A. for a few weeks. He was always tense and nervous lately, and he spent as much time huddled over his computer as she spent huddled over her history books. She didn't understand exactly what he did with computers, but she knew he was very good at it. Like his mother, Mordred was brilliant and rather peculiar.

Realizing that she'd been silent longer than was polite, Leah glanced up at Adam's face. He was extremely rugged looking, an unusual trait in academics. His skin glowed with a healthy tan, his hair was streaked by the sun and his well-muscled shoulders tapered down to narrow hips and a flat belly.

"Verbena tells me she admires your writing," Leah said to keep the conversation going.

"In some ways. We disagree on certain salient points of writing a history book."

His eyes were his most remarkable feature, she decided. They were a bright, pale blue. Warm and lively, they could probably appear cold and icy when he was angry. They brought out the obvious intelligence in his strong features and echoed the casual, irreverent attitude of his broad smile and relaxed body.

"Do you mean you have different theories about your subject?" she asked.

"No, we have slightly different ideas about how to present our theories and about who our audience should be."

His voice was deep and slightly raspy. He didn't speak with the precise enunciation or slow, deliberate phrasing of many of her male colleagues.

"Did you read Verbena's last book?" Leah asked.

He nodded. His look gave nothing away. "Did you?"

"Of course." Her eyes met his. Then for some reason she admitted, "Well, only half of it actually." She saw amusement in Adam's blue eyes as she rushed on to explain, "I have to read so much material, and her book wasn't directly related to the work I'm doing now, though of course—"

"I know, I know, you don't have to explain," he interrupted with a smile. He suspected that, like most people, she hadn't been able to plow all the way through it but felt it was disloyal to admit that. "I was a doctoral student, too. You read so much it starts to swim past your eyes after a while, and you're not even sure how you know what you know."

"That's a perfect description of my mental state. Summer came just in time for me."

"Don't tell me you came *here* for rest and relaxation? Do you have any idea what kind of manpower it takes to feed all these animals?"

"I remember. On the other hand, I love Verbena and like to visit her when I can. Except for her private zoo, it's usually quiet and peaceful out here. Verbena has one of the best personal libraries in the country, and she can get me into the libraries at Cornell and Ithaca College if there's any other research I need to do. What's more, she feeds me."

"That's a dubious advantage, considering her cooking," Adam said in a low voice.

"Maybe I should rephrase that. Let's just say the food is free."

"So you came here to work on your thesis all summer?"

"That's right," said Leah, looking into those crystal-clear blue eyes set in a strong intelligent face framed by a cloud of wavy golden hair. "I came here to work in peace and quiet without any distractions."

"Yeah, me too," Adam said softly.

Their eyes met. Who were they kidding, Adam thought wryly. They were already distracting each other. His eyes held Leah's for longer than was polite, wondering what she possessed that was already attracting him so strongly, despite a lack of spontaneous warmth on her part.

Leah broke the spell by sighing and looking away. She tried to continue their conversation in an impersonal social tone, hoping he didn't notice the inexplicable breathlessness that had entered her normally smooth voice.

"Well, considering your relative youth, it's quite an opportunity to collaborate with Verbena."

"It's an honor," Adam admitted readily. "I was flattered when she approached me. I can honestly say it's the first time in my life I was speechless. She's practically a living legend in our field."

"She is a great teacher."

"She really is. I'm learning a lot by working with her. I guess I felt pretty smug after a few successful books, but she's humbled me again. She always had that effect on me," he added wryly.

Leah propped her chin on her hand and looked at him, liking his apparent respect and affection for Verbena, his patience with her aunt's menagerie and his friendliness. She liked the humility that could creep into his cocky self-confidence. Perhaps she shouldn't be so automatically protective of her aunt. Perhaps she was wrong to have suspected, even for a moment, that he had used his charm in place of solid credentials to form a partnership with Verbena.

Then she did a double take. "A few successful books?"

He nodded.

"Maybe I've read them," she said hopefully.

She wondered why he hesitated ever so slightly before responding. "Maybe."

"What name do you publish under?"

"My own."

"What's your full name?"

"Adam Jordan."

"Adam Jor..." Leah lost her voice before she was done speaking his name. Her eyes widened and she swallowed.

"You recognize it?" he asked. His slightly cynical tone seemed to confirm what she had to ask anyway.

"*Reach for the Scepter*, *His Majesty's Pleasure*, *They Also Serve*—you're *that* Adam Jordan?" Leah asked, her expression begging him to deny it.

"That's me," he confirmed, absolutely deadpan.

Leah stared at him, aghast. Adam Jordan was the antithesis of the respectable scholar. A flashy, slick author of bestselling history books that were so padded with speculation and supposition they didn't even deserve to be labeled nonfiction, let alone historical studies.

Regrettably, Leah said the first thing that came into her head. "Verbena asked *you* to collaborate with her? Has she lost her mind?"

Adam frowned, and a sudden, stormy expression swept across his face. "Who the hell do you—"

"Here we are!" Verbena appeared in the doorway with a tray of coffee.

There was a sudden howl of rage in the kitchen. The ferret ran between Verbena's feet with Macbeth, the collie, in hot pursuit.

"Macbeth! No!" Adam jumped to his feet, already seeing the ensuing disaster in his mind.

Leah shot out of her chair and tripped over the Questing Beast as he nervously skittered past her. She fell facedown on the hard floor and lay there, winded.

Inevitably Macbeth followed King John's path between Verbena's feet, all ninety pounds of him going at full speed. Verbena flew up into the air. The contents of the coffee tray flew past Leah's prostrate body and crashed against the wall. Macbeth chased King John in a frantic circle around the room, knocking over several chairs.

Adam helped Verbena to her feet. "One of these days, Verbena, one of your own damned watchdogs is going to be the death of you."

"Collies aren't watchdogs. Collies are—"

"Never mind," he said patiently. His eyes met Leah's as she scrambled to her feet. His look was ironic. "Peace and quiet, you said?"

Two

Leah decided she would obviously have to talk to Verbena about this ill-advised collaboration with the notorious Adam Jordan. As far as Leah was concerned, he was entirely the wrong person to help her aunt recover her confidence after the heavy criticism of her last book. In fact, he was perhaps the only person Verbena could have chosen who could completely ruin and discredit the lofty academic reputation she had built over the course of nearly forty years in the field.

I've been away too long, Leah thought guiltily. Everything at home had gone to pot. There was an iguana, a ferret and heaven only knew what else running loose in the house. The house itself needed painting, cleaning and numerous repairs. And Adam Jordan, the scourge of respectable academia, had moved in and set himself up as Verbena's new collaborator.

"It's like the Book of Job," Leah muttered distractedly as she wiped coffee stains off the dining-room wall. "What else could go wrong?"

"Coming through," said Adam with insufferable good cheer as he edged around Leah with a mop and bucket.

"Auntie, what happened to Jenny Harper?" During her past visit, Leah had arranged for a woman to clean the house twice a week and go grocery shopping at least once a week. Verbena would otherwise work cheerfully caked in dust and consume nothing but junk food and heavily sugared coffee.

"She quit."

"Can't imagine why," said Adam blandly.

Leah shot him a look of irritation before asking her aunt why.

"It was so peculiar, dear. She claimed the house was haunted."

Leah stared at Verbena blankly, refusing to let Adam see how much his amusement annoyed her. She cleared her throat. "She actually said she was quitting because the house was *haunted*?"

"Hmm."

"How long ago was that?"

"This winter."

"Good grief, Auntie," Leah exclaimed, troubled by the image of her aged aunt trying to keep this enormous, pet-filled house clean all by herself. "Why on earth didn't you hire someone else?"

"No one else was willing to come to work for me."

Leah sat back on her heels as they finished cleaning up the mess. "Why not?" Her aunt was the most generous, friendly person alive.

Verbena frowned briefly. "They say I have too many pets."

Leah had no response to that.

"Nonsense!" Adam grinned and stooped to kiss the top of Verbena's head with a familiarity that Leah found totally inappropriate.

As Leah helped Verbena to her feet, her aunt glanced hopefully at her. "Now that you're home, perhaps you can find someone. Or better yet, maybe you could convince Jenny Harper to come back to work for me. All the pets adored her, you know. She's the first cleaning woman who didn't mutter all the time about what a mess they make."

Leah sighed. "I'll see what I can do, Auntie."

Verbena smiled angelically and squeezed Leah's hand. "There's also a stack of legal letters and bank statements and that sort of stuff in the study. You know I don't have any gift for that kind of thing." Her dark eyes sparkled as Leah agreed to take care of it.

Leah had definitely been away too long and had her work cut out for her. She fully intended to broach the subject of Verbena's new collaborator when she and her aunt had a moment alone together, but fatigue and a sense of inevitability suddenly overwhelmed her. It could wait until tomorrow, surely.

After cleaning up the dining room and washing the dinner dishes, Leah agreed that she'd like to unpack her things and take a long, soothing bath. Adam offered to carry her suitcase upstairs. The two women followed silently behind him.

Leah was distracted by the play of Adam's muscles as he heaved her book-laden suitcase up the long, wide staircase to the second floor. His impressive display of biceps and deltoids merely confirmed her conviction that he'd never spent five minutes inside a library, she decided sourly.

Verbena was occupied with comforting the distraught King John, who nestled against her as she cradled him in her arms. Macbeth followed at her heels, eyeing the ferret with open dislike.

When they reached the upstairs hallway, Adam stumbled slightly on the corner of a Persian rug covering the smooth wooden floor. Taking this as a signal for a game to commence, Macbeth pounced on him from behind and tried to trip him again.

"Cut it out," said Adam mildly, already accustomed to the many hazards of living in Verbena's house.

"Oh, dear, calm down," said Verbena as the ferret twisted nervously in her arms.

Leaving Adam and Verbena occupied with their furry companions, Leah carried her small overnight bag down the big hallway to the familiar room she always stayed in. She opened the door and stopped abruptly.

The place was a mess. The bed was unmade, someone's clothes were scattered haphazardly everywhere, every surface was piled high with books, notebooks, papers, magazines and newspapers, half a dozen coffee mugs and a few empty bags of junk food were perched around the room, a sheet of paper was sticking out of the typewriter on the desk and some fifty sheets of crumpled paper lay scattered on the floor by the wastebasket.

"Good Lord, what's happened here?" she exclaimed.

Although she had cleared this room of all personal possessions when she had moved west several years ago, Leah nonetheless continued to think of it as *her* room. Seeing it violated this way shocked her.

"Leah!" Adam called, coming down the hallway, carrying her suitcase with one hand and holding a squirming Macbeth by the scuff of the neck with the other. He halted at the doorway of her vandalized room. "Oh, here you are."

Her expression of outrage warned him that something was seriously wrong. "What happened in here?" she demanded.

"Is this your old room?" he asked hesitantly.

"Yes. And it's never looked like this!" Her dark eyes flashed back to him. "*You're* staying in here?"

Adam nearly winced. She'd be an intimidating history professor once she got her degree. He could just picture freshman boys cowering before her beautiful but stern expression as they tried to explain why their papers were overdue.

"Yes. I'm sorry, Leah. When I arrived, Verbena gave me my pick of the rooms, and I chose this one because it had the most room to spread out in."

Leah looked around the room without bothering to hide her distaste. She liked to work and sleep in a clean, ordered atmosphere and couldn't understand this kind of sloth. Her expression told him so.

"Well, since you're already in here, I suppose I'll use one of the other bedrooms," Leah said at last.

"Oh, dear, this *is* the room you usually use, isn't it?" said Verbena, who had entered the room as Leah made her last comment. "I didn't even think about that. How remiss of me."

"That's all right, Auntie. You didn't know then that I would be coming home, and you have too many things on your mind to—"

"I'll move, of course," Adam offered. He sensed there would be trouble enough between him and Leah without adding to it unnecessarily. He wondered how long it would take him to shift all his belongings and papers to another room.

"No, that's all right," said Leah politely.

"Really, I insist. If this is your favorite room—"

"No. Forget it, really," said Leah. It would take a week of cleaning to make this room habitable, she thought fastidiously. In addition to being a crass commercial hack, Adam Jordan was also a slob.

Leah looked longingly at the bed for a moment—the only bed in the whole house that wasn't a water bed—and turned to leave the room.

As she pivoted, her heel slipped on something. She looked down and saw she was stepping on an envelope. She bent over quickly and picked it up. "Is this yours?"

Adam casually took the envelope from her and tossed it onto the overflowing desk, but not before she had seen the return address: Lavish Books, in New York City. Hardly a scholarly publisher. Her eyes flashed up to his face in surprise.

"Nothing important," he said. He met her snapping eyes with a bland expression. He'd be damned if he'd offer explanations of excuses to her about something that was none of her business. Young Miss McCargar's freely distributed disapproval was beginning to wear down his patience, and she had only been in the house a few hours. It was a shame she didn't seem to have a personality that matched the warm good looks she'd been gifted with.

"I suppose taking another room really is the wisest course of action," said Verbena cheerfully. "Adam appears to be quite ensconced in this one."

"Indeed," said Leah icily.

"Why don't you use the yellow room, dear? It has a wonderful view of the backyard."

"All right, Auntie. Sorry to have intruded," she added to Adam, who was still standing in front of the desk and obviously waiting for her to leave. The speculative look in his eyes bothered her.

"No intrusion at all." He smiled his most charming smile as Verbena and Leah exited the room. As soon as the door was closed behind them, he plopped into a chair and began going over Verbena's notes. After reading a page three times in a row without absorbing a single word of it, he tossed the notes aside and leaned back in his chair.

He stretched, closed his eyes and let his thoughts dwell on Verbena's lovely and exasperating niece.

She was a study in contrasts: dark hair and pale skin, slim lines and lush curves, hot looks and cold words. She was warm and loving toward Verbena. Indeed, during the course of the evening she had exhibited more patience than could reasonably be expected of anyone when dealing with her eccentric aunt. The way Verbena was already dumping responsibilities onto Leah indicated that she was accustomed to relying on that gentle aspect of her niece's character.

Leah had reacted negatively to him, however, from the moment she'd laid eyes on him. That puzzled him. And her condescending attitude toward him once she realized who he was touched a sore spot.

He smiled wryly. He should be above such petty pain by now, but he wasn't. He had wanted to be a respected historian since his senior year in high school. He loved the puzzles and mysteries of the past, the dusty library shelves and the thin yellowed pages of old history books, the thread of individual stories running through the great events that had shaped the world.

Despite his reputation, he had once treated the academic world with respect, fully expecting to be a part of it, until that day at Barrington University six years ago, when he had submitted his doctoral dissertation to his advisor.

He wondered again, as he had so many times since entering Verbena's personal and professional domain, if he should come clean with her. He took a deep breath and tried to relax.

Tomorrow, he vowed. Tomorrow he would tell her the truth.

Leah awoke the next morning feeling groggy and disoriented. She turned her head gently and set a tidal wave in motion.

"Ohh," she moaned unhappily as the water bed in the yellow room sloshed and rolled.

Verbena had had a mania about water beds and their beneficial effects on the spine since Leah's teenage years. Mordred had insisted they keep at least one "real" bed in the house. Leah had convinced Verbena to keep the real bed in her old room, and she and Mordred had fought over it ever since, each devising cunning ways to cheat the other out of that room during their visits home.

Of course, Mordred usually won since Leah was unable to refuse him anything. Although they were of an age, she had always protected Mordred and taken responsibility for him.

So while the misery of sleeping on a water bed was nothing new to Leah, she thought that maybe she should have taken Adam up on his offer to switch rooms.

Gathering all her strength, Leah tried to push herself up. The bed squished down below her elbows and water rose in a vast wave under her hips, putting her in an uncomfortable and ridiculous position. Verbena wasn't keeping enough water in this bed, Leah thought irritably. That was something else she would have to see to today.

Muttering to herself, she fell back against the pillows. The mattress heaved around her for several minutes. After it had finally stilled, she thought she might have a chance for escape if she crawled to the side of the bed and threw herself to the floor.

She rolled over onto her stomach, but was immediately thrown back onto her posterior by the resultant motion of water in response to her actions. She might have had a fighting chance if she'd weighed twenty pounds more, but at the moment matters looked hopeless. How on earth did Verbena, a small woman in her sixties, manage to get out of one of these fiendish contraptions every day?

With great relief she heard unsteady footsteps pass in the hallway. She'd already wasted ten minutes of the day just trying to get out of bed. Time for serious measures.

"Help!" she cried. "Auntie! Please help me!"

The door flew open. Adam was standing on the other side of it. There was a long moment of silence while they regarded each other. He had clearly just awoken. He wore cotton shorts and a wrinkled tank top, his hair was rumpled and curly and his face was dark with the beginnings of a beard.

His eyes, more than any other feature, were what gave him away. Bleary and unfocused, they looked at her with bewilderment and an absolute lack of recognition. He stared at her, clearly dumbfounded, for several more moments.

Finally in a low, fuzzy voice he said, "Verbena's niece, right?"

Leah nodded, not sure how to handle the situation.

"Leah?" he asked.

"Yes, that's right," she said encouragingly.

"Calling for help," he mumbled.

"I can't get out of bed," she explained, feeling ridiculous.

He frowned. "Why not?"

She shrugged, then floundered helplessly in the waves produced by this action.

"Wow," he said, clearly impressed. "Get any sleep?"

"A little. Adam, do you think you could . . . ?"

"Oh, sure." He stumbled forward, his every motion lacking the natural grace of the night before. He was obviously not a morning person.

"Give me your hands," he ordered. She did so, placing her smooth white hands in his firm grasp. She winced at the unconscious strength of his grip; sleep obviously didn't affect his basic reflexes.

Adam braced one leg against the padded roll that bordered the side of the bed. "Wait a minute, you'll trip." He released her hands and leaned forward to rip the sheet off her body.

Leah gasped, startled by the speed and aggression of his movement. She lay beneath his gaze in a modest cotton nightgown, which had slipped enough to show a generous amount of shoulder and thigh. He stared at her with intense concentration, and she could now see alert awareness enter his expression with amazing speed.

Waking up much faster than usual, Adam let his gaze roam over the beautiful woman stretched out before him. Her dark hair was spread across the pillow and fell around her shoulders in sharp contrast to the smooth, creamy whiteness of her skin. Her cotton gown hid everything and yet provocatively hinted at a lushness beneath its folds that boggled the mind. Her long legs, smooth, slim and firm, slid suggestively against the sheets as she tried unsuccessfully to sit up. Her motion created a gentle heaving in the bed, which somehow added to the eroticism growing inside him.

Realizing that he was making her nervous, he groggily said, "You're very pretty," and straightened up to yank her out of bed without warning.

Thrown off balance by the sudden change of position, Leah fell against Adam in a little heap. He threw his arms around her and braced himself to keep them both from falling.

Leah settled her feet firmly on the floor, took a deep breath and pushed at Adam's chest. It was like pushing at a wall of granite.

"Adam, you can let go now," she said clearly.

"In a minute," he murmured.

He nestled her head against his shoulder and rested his cheek on top of her hair. Leah's eyes widened in surprise. Smothered against him, she assessed the situation. He had gone absolutely still, making no attempt to touch her more seductively or urge her back into bed.

His embrace was too intimate for comfort, considering they'd only just met, but it was affectionate rather than sexual, and since she had invited him into her bedroom—in a manner of speaking—Leah found she couldn't take offense.

In fact, if she were honest, she rather enjoyed it. His body was pleasantly warm, his embrace cozy and relaxing. He smelled musky from sleep, and his body felt strong and slim and heavy. He seemed to be getting heavier by the second, actually.

"Adam?" Steady, deep breathing was the only response. "Adam?" She squeezed his arm.

"Hmm?" he moaned groggily.

"Adam, wake up!" she insisted, pinching him sharply.

"Ow!" He seized her shoulders and pushed her just far enough away to glare at her. "What! What?" he demanded belligerently.

"You were falling back asleep," she said tersely, feeling perversely insulted.

"Oh." He ran a hand through his hair. His eyes raked her accusingly. "Why are you so tidy?"

"What?"

"Why isn't your hair messy? Why aren't your eyes puffy? Why isn't your nightgown wrinkled?" he demanded.

"I ... don't know," she said, bewildered.

"You were like that yesterday, too," he continued irritably. "It's an all-day trip from Palo Alto, but you looked perfect when you got here."

"Thank you. I think."

He glared at her again. "It's not normal. What sort of a person are you?" he said insultingly and then stomped out the door.

"Where are you going?" she demanded.

"Shower," he muttered as he plodded down the hall.

Leah stared after him for a moment and then closed the door and leaned back against it. She looked around the room as if she could find some clue to explain the scene that had just occurred there.

"What a way to start the day," she muttered at last. In addition to being disreputable and messy, Verbena's collaborator was also unpredictable. Was there no end to the man's flaws?

In the midst of the morning's chores, Leah found no time to discuss the subject uppermost in her mind. Following a quick breakfast, she drove Verbena into town to pick up groceries and cleaning supplies. They also spent a half hour at the feed-and-seed supplier buying food for Verbena's menagerie, as well as for all the local wildlife she fed. "My goodness, Auntie, it's a wonder you haven't gone broke feeding all those monsters," said Leah as they drove home.

"They do eat a lot," Verbena admitted. "But it's money well spent. We can't let them go hungry, after all. And I can afford it."

Which was true. Leah didn't know the exact figures, but she knew that between Verbena's university salary, royalties from past books, payments for her contributions to other people's books and speaking and lecture fees, her aunt made quite a comfortable living.

As Leah drove home, Verbena leafed through her pocket calendar to see what other chores she had planned for the day. "Oh, dear!" she exclaimed suddenly.

"What's wrong?"

"I completely forgot, Melchior Browning is coming over for lunch today. How remiss of me."

"Professor Browning? Author of *Social Ramifications of Mystery Plays in the Reign of Henry VI*?"

"Yes."

"How exciting, Auntie! That book helped inspire the topic of my thesis. It'll be a pleasure to meet him."

"I hope so," said Verbena with a worried frown.

"What's wrong?" Leah slowed the car and turned down a road leading out of town.

"Melchior doesn't like animals much. Actually he loathes them."

"I see."

"What's more, it's mutual. The pets just *hate* him for some reason."

"Really?" Leah pondered the problem. With a collie, two Shih Tzus, two Siamese cats, a ferret, an iguana, a mynah bird and at least four extra unidentified cats she had noticed running around this morning, there were too many bodies to keep track of. No guest could be guaranteed safe conduct through the house if he and the menagerie didn't get along.

"That's not all," said Verbena, eagerly laying the rest of her dilemma at Leah's feet.

"There's more?"

"Keep your eyes on the road, dear."

"You of all people shouldn't tell me how to drive," Leah reminded her. "What else are you worried about?"

"Melchior and Adam don't seem to like each other at all."

"No?"

"In fact, I think it's fair to say they treat each other with open hostility at times."

"Is that a fact?" said Leah curiously.

"I just don't understand why two such intelligent people can't get along," Verbena fretted, conveniently forgetting the raging arguments she often had with other historians, and even with her own son on occasion. Leah let it pass.

"I hate to mention it, but Adam seemed to be in a very peculiar mood today," Leah said.

"You saw him this morning?"

"Yes. He's quite mercurial, isn't he?"

"Actually, he's very even tempered most of the time. But he's definitely not a morning person. I sometimes think he doesn't know his own name before he's had a shower and a cup of coffee. He must have been especially foul tempered this morning, too."

"Why do you say that?" Leah asked, thinking back to his strange behavior.

"The two Shih Tzus, T'ai and Chi, woke me up for an emergency walk in the middle of the night, and I could hear Adam's typewriter going full steam ahead."

"He works on *A Viable Alternative* at night?"

"He pretty much works whenever inspiration strikes him, and he doesn't stop till he drops from exhaustion or runs out of ideas, whichever comes first."

"Seems very impractical to me," Leah said critically as she turned into Verbena's driveway.

"One mustn't question genius," said Verbena placidly as they pulled to a stop.

"Adam Jordan is hardly a genius. No, don't get out. I want to talk to you about him, as long as we're on the subject."

"But the groceries will go bad—"

"In five minutes?"

"And the pets are probably terribly hungry by now, dear." Verbena hopped out of the car with remarkable speed and agility for a woman of her age.

"This will only take—"

"Perhaps it was unwise of me to invite Melchior today. You *will* help me make sure it's a pleasant afternoon, won't you, dear?"

"Of course I will. Only—" Leah stopped speaking abruptly as Verbena shoved two large, heavy bags of groceries into her arms. She decided to give up for the moment. She had the suspicious feeling that Verbena knew what she wanted to say and specifically wanted to avoid talking about it.

She carried her burden up the front porch and kicked on the door, hoping Adam would hear her. He flung the door open only moments later.

"Where's the ferret?" she said automatically.

"Backyard. Whadjya bring me?" said Adam, peering into the grocery bags as Leah thrust them into his arms.

"Half the fresh produce in western New York. You unload the car. I'll put things away in the kitchen."

"And who'll keep Verbena out of trouble?"

"Very funny." But she felt the corners of her mouth turn up as she pushed her way past him and headed toward the kitchen.

Half an hour later Adam had emptied the car, Leah had filled up the kitchen cupboards and Verbena had fed a bevy of beasts on the back porch. With everything apparently under control for the moment, Leah cornered Verbena in the sun-filled study, ignoring the mynah bird who made rude suggestions in Middle English.

"Auntie, can we talk now?"

"Well, actually—"

Both women fell silent as Adam stomped into the room. His handsome face was free of its already familiar good humor. He looked grave, sober and full of resolution.

"Verbena, I have to talk to you."

Leah glanced at him in surprise. "Can it wait?"

Adam was reluctant to let his subterfuge go on for even another moment. He should have told Verbena right from the start. Now was the time to have it out. "No, I'm afraid not."

Looking from one to the other, Verbena apparently came to a resolution of her own. "Adam, dear, I want you to brace yourself."

He looked surprised. "Brace myself? For what?"

Verbena took a deep breath and then said in a rush, "Melchior Browning is coming here for lunch today, and I want you to be nice to him."

Leah had yet to see Adam look so stormy. "Browning? Coming here? What for?" Verbena was right. Adam's dislike vibrated powerfully through his low voice, and the man hadn't even arrived yet.

Leah frowned at him. "He's a friend and colleague of my aunt's, that's what for," she said repressively. The nerve!

Adam made a visible effort to control his temper. After a moment of tense silence he said, "Of course I'll be polite to him, Verbena. He and I are both your guests."

"I knew I could count on you." Verbena smiled tremulously. Leah wasn't so sure. "Now what was it you wanted to discuss with me?"

He looked blank for a moment, then his dark brows swooped down again.

"Adam?" Verbena prompted.

"I..." He shrugged his shoulders and looked away. "It's not important, Verbena."

Leah exchanged a doubtful glance with her aunt. Despite what Verbena had said earlier, she still considered Adam mercurial. He turned to go, but stilled at the sound of Verbena's voice.

"Could I impose upon you to cook lunch for all of us, Adam? You know how inadequate I am in the kitchen."

He raised one arm against the doorjamb and let his head drop forward. In that position, with the rays of the late-morning sun glinting off his dark golden hair and lighter golden skin, he looked like a pagan god to Leah.

His shoulders started to shake, and for a breathless moment Leah wondered if something was wrong with him. Then she realized with astonishment that he was laughing.

His voice choked with rueful amusement, Adam said, "No one but you could get away with asking that, Verbena." He turned to cast Leah a sparkling look before saying, "Except maybe your niece."

With that parting shot, he disappeared down the hallway, shaking his head and chuckling to himself.

Three

Verbena locked herself in her study to catch up on correspondence with scholars around the world, and to answer invitations to lecture at various institutes. Leah filled up her water bed, then called the roofers, the plumbers, the chimney sweeps and the housepainters. Then, wanting to look respectable for the eminent scholar who would be visiting them that afternoon, she showered and changed into an attractive cotton dress of violet, aqua and indigo.

Adam's eyes roved over her with open flattery as she entered the kitchen. He let out a low whistle and raised his brows. "Very nice, Miss McCargar. Is this all for our visiting professor?"

He was wearing faded cutoffs and a gray tank top. His curly golden hair was rumpled, and his shoes looked old and comfortable. "Certainly. And are you dressing down for the occasion?" she inquired crisply.

He grinned. "No. It's nothing personal. I don't dress up for anybody."

"Ever?"

He tilted his head to admire her sleek chignon. "Well, if I thought you'd gone to that much trouble with your hair for *my* sake, I might reconsider." She jerked away when he raised a hand to stroke her hair. He leaned forward and confided, "Of course, if Kathleen Turner or Sophia Loren were coming for lunch, I guess I'd make an effort."

"Yes, well, things being what they are, you won't need to waste any time changing, will you?" She handed him a pot.

He regarded it dubiously and then cocked a brow at her. "I don't suppose you can cook?"

"I'll make the salad." She purposely avoided answering his question. She didn't mind letting him do all the cooking for a little while longer.

Adam sighed and filled the pot with water. He added a dash of salt and set it on the stove to boil. "Sleep well?"

Leah raised both brows and looked at him expectantly.

"What?" he asked.

"You've already asked me that."

"No, I haven't."

"This morning."

Adam looked blank for a moment, then realization slowly dawned, spreading across his face and widening his blue eyes. "I vaguely remember now. Something about you...stuck in bed." He grinned suddenly. "You're very fetching in that little cotton nightie."

"It's not little. It's very modest," Leah said confidently, remembering nonetheless how his gaze had seemed to burn through the pale material.

Adam leaned very close to her and let his gaze roam over her features. There was a wicked glint in his eyes. "Ah, but I have an excellent imagination. Much aided, may I say, by your tempting—"

"What are you making for lunch?" Leah interrupted, embarrassed.

He grinned, enjoying her apparent discomfort. She may not like him, but she wasn't entirely indifferent. "Pasta primavera."

"Again?" She heard the breathlessness in her own voice. The look in his eyes let her know he had heard it, too. She didn't think a man's mere physical presence had affected her this much since her hopeless adolescent crush on the high-school football star.

"I'm afraid it's my only company dish. I'm only a great cook in comparison to Verbena."

Hoping to slow down her racing pulse, Leah moved over to the sink and began washing lettuce. "I take it you didn't sleep well?" she asked at last. There were faint smudges under his eyes and lines of weariness at their corners.

"No, but I got a lot of work done." He smiled sheepishly at her. "I'm afraid, however, that whatever I may have said or done this morning is pretty typical. I'm scarcely human the first hour I'm awake."

Leah smiled with remembered amusement. "Must be hard on your—" She stopped herself.

"Girlfriends?" he supplied.

She nodded, concentrating on separating and washing the lettuce.

"There isn't one now," he volunteered.

She glanced at him, feeling like doing a little teasing herself. "Do they leave you one by one after they can't put up with your morning moods anymore?"

"Most women have told me I'm rather endearing in the mornings," he said loftily as he poured some olive oil into a saucepan.

"Perhaps they were being polite." She began tearing up the lettuce and dropping little tidbits down to the Questing Beast, who lurked at her feet and watched her intently.

"I did help you escape your bed this morning, didn't I? I'm not all that bad, even at my worst."

The phone rang. Adam answered it. "Hello? Yes. Shall I get Verbena? Oh . . . sure." He handed the receiver to Leah.

"It's Mordred. He doesn't want to talk to Verbena. Just you."

Leah's heart pounded with both relief and anticipation. Maybe now she could get some answers from her cousin. She wiped her hands and took the receiver. "Hello?"

"Leah! Thank God you're there!" Her cousin's familiar voice was frantic.

"What's wrong, Mordred? Where are you?"

"Never mind where I am! I haven't got much time, so listen closely."

"What are you talking about?" she asked.

"What did you tell Mother?"

"I told her you were delayed. And listen, Mordred—"

He interrupted her. "Who else have you told?"

"What?"

"Who else?" he demanded.

"Well . . ." She glanced across the room. Adam was slicing vegetables and had his back to her. "No one," she said at last.

"You're sure?"

"What are you—"

"Listen, Leah. Tell everyone I'm not coming!"

"What? Mordred, we agreed, you promised—"

"I *am* coming! Just tell everyone that I'm not."

"I don't understand," said Leah, bewildered.

"No time to explain now. Just do it. And say nothing about this conversation. Nothing! I'll see you later."

"Mordred!" The line had gone dead.

Leah held the receiver away from her face and stared at it in confusion. Adam, who had turned around to look at her with concern, gently took the receiver away from her and hung up the phone.

"Is something wrong?" he asked.

Leah looked at Adam, looked at the phone, then looked at Adam again. She opened her mouth and closed it.

Say nothing, Mordred had said.

How ridiculous.

She started to say something to Adam, then hesitated. Until she had had time to think this over, perhaps saying nothing would be the best course of action, after all.

"Leah?" he prompted.

"No. Nothing's wrong," she said at last.

"That sounded . . . peculiar."

"Oh, you know Mordred," she said lightly, going back to the sink to finish preparing the lettuce.

"No, I don't." He clearly wasn't convinced.

"Isn't your water boiling yet?"

"Has something happened that will affect Verbena?"

Leah studied him for a moment, appreciating his concern for her aunt's welfare. "I have no idea," she said. Which was true. She didn't know what Mordred was up to.

"Leah."

"Do you hear someone knocking at the front door? Maybe Professor Browning has arrived."

She left the kitchen hurriedly, leaving Adam staring after her with a thoughtful frown on his face.

As Leah walked through the house to the entrance hall, she wondered if she should keep quiet about Mordred's call. She didn't like keeping his call a secret, but that had seemed extremely important to him.

She had been through this sort of thing with Mordred before. Several years ago she discovered that he had long since dropped out of his M.A. program and was spending the tuition money Verbena sent him on wine, women and song. She had straightened out that mess and never told Verbena; the damage was done and her aunt could only be hurt by hindsight.

She had sworn to Mordred that that was the last time she was ever going to help him out of a mess. But in a brilliant and eccentric family, Leah had taken responsibility for others for so long that it was second nature to her.

What's more, she never again wanted to experience the pain of disappointing her loved ones and not having the chance to make amends. She could never let down Verbena or Mordred. They were all she had. She supposed Mordred knew that whatever he was involved in this time, she would straighten things out to keep Verbena—and him—from getting hurt.

She heard Adam's footsteps coming swiftly behind her as she approached the front door. His face was set in tense lines, but she still felt a momentary twinge of envy as her eyes met his.

It must be nice not to have anything on your conscience, she thought.

Having come from the study, Verbena beat Leah to the front door and opened it herself to greet their guest. Leah found Professor Melchior Browning's appearance as impressive as his reputation. Somewhere in his mid-fifties, he carried himself with aristocratic stature. He was of medium height and build, with neatly brushed brown hair that included a dignified amount of gray. His moustache, goatee beard and tweed jacket with elbow patches completed the visual picture of a scholarly gentleman.

He greeted her aunt with charming deference, so unlike the wryly affectionate familiarity that Adam expressed toward Verbena.

"This is my niece, Leah. She's working on her Ph.D. at Stanford," Verbena said proudly.

Professor Browning took Leah's hand and raised it toward his face in a courtly gesture. He didn't kiss it; that would have been extravagant. Nevertheless, he made Leah feel feminine and flattered. She smiled and murmured a polite greeting, vaguely conscious of Adam glowering nearby.

"Of course Verbena has mentioned you," Professor Browning said in elegant, cultured tones reminiscent of the British royal family. "She is terribly proud of you, my dear. In fact, she has so praised your intellectual capabilities that she neglected to mention how lovely you are."

"Thank you." Leah smiled with pleasure. Adam ruined the moment by rolling his eyes heavenward behind Professor Browning. "I believe you know my aunt's colleague, Adam Jordan," she said, gesturing in Adam's direction.

Professor Browning turned toward Adam, and Leah noticed the subtle change in his expression. He clearly didn't like Adam any better than Adam liked him.

"Ah, yes. Verbena mentioned that you were enjoying her hospitality, Mr. Jordan."

Leah shifted uncomfortably, feeling a little surprised. The comment bordered on rudeness since Professor Browning's tone clearly implied that *all* Adam was doing here was enjoying Verbena's famous hospitality.

Adam didn't seem surprised by the implied slur. In fact, he smiled. Not the broad, irreverent grin Leah had already grown accustomed to, but a small, cynical smile. "That's *Dr.* Jordan, to *you*," he said flatly.

There was an embarrassed silence. Then Leah and Verbena began speaking at once as the two men stood facing each other, both evidently unwilling to back down from some private challenge.

Exerting the full force of her charm, Verbena took control of the situation before anything seriously antisocial could happen. She hustled Adam back into the kitchen, escorted Leah and Professor Browning into the dining room and poured iced tea for everyone. She, Leah and the professor were all chatting amicably when Adam finally brought out their lunch. Leah didn't offer to help him. She had already surmised that Verbena had asked him to make lunch for an ulterior motive, one with which she wholeheartedly agreed; the more time Adam spent out of Professor Browning's company today, the better.

Pasta primavera might be Adam's only "company" dish, but he did it very well. Verbena's compliments were florid. Leah suspected she was trying to show Professor Browning that Adam was important to her. The strategy worked in that it forced Professor Browning to comment politely on the meal. This led to some reasonably civil dialogue between the two men.

"Where are you based these days?" Professor Browning asked.

Adam twisted spaghetti around his fork. "In Boston. And you?"

"The same old place."

"And where is that?" Leah asked.

"Barrington, Connecticut."

"Barrington?" Leah suddenly made the connection. "Of course! You're the head of the history department there, aren't you?"

"Yes."

Leah was vaguely aware of her aunt contorting her face into a peculiar expression, but she ignored it to pursue her next question. "Adam, didn't you say you were at Barrington for your Ph.D. work?"

Adam's eyes met Professor Browning's for a moment. "That's right."

"Were you there then, Professor? Is that how you two know each other?"

"Yes."

There was an uncomfortable silence. Leah wondered why neither man chose to elaborate. If Adam had been a doctoral student there for three years, they must have been more than passing acquaintances. She looked at each of them expectantly for a short moment before she realized that, judging by the expressions on their faces, neither of them had happy memories of their association in those years. Perhaps their mutual antipathy went back that far, she mused.

Struggling to keep the conversation going, Leah said, "I must tell you how much I admire your work, Professor." She had actually only read his most recent book. It was responsible and scholarly, although he had uncovered no new evidence and drawn no new conclusions.

"Please," he interrupted, holding up his hand, "you make me feel like an old man. I insist you call me Melchior."

"Melchior," she amended, aware of the sardonic light in Adam's eyes across the table. "Your work on fifteenth-century religious plays helped inspire the theme for my thesis." He had only mentioned her subject in a general way in his book, but that was when she had first become interested in it.

"Really? I am flattered. And so pleased to have inspired a young scholar."

"In fact, perhaps you could offer me some advice." It never hurt to ask for help from a renowned professor.

"I'd be only too glad to, my dear."

"My topic concerns political radicalism disguised as religious morality in mystery plays during the worst outbreaks of the Black Death in the fourteenth century."

"Hmm, yes, yes, indeed, an interesting topic. I should be very glad to advise you, my dear. What is it you need?"

"Well, I've already found a lot of excellent governmental and ecclesiastical documentation, but I'm still looking for direct source material about some of the actual players involved in such controversy."

"Hmm. Yes, yes, indeed. Such sources are extremely rare."

He frowningly pondered the question for such a long time that Leah wondered if her task would be hopeless. "Do you think there's any chance at all that you can help me?"

"It will take me some time, but I'm sure I can come up with something." He patted her hand reassuringly.

"More pasta, Verbena?" Adam said loudly across the table.

"Yes, thank you, dear." Leah saw Verbena give Adam a warning frown and wondered what it meant.

"Leah? No, I see you've barely touched your plate. Professor?" Adam inquired solicitously.

"Just a bit more. Got to watch my weight, you know," he added with a self-deprecating smile.

"I think you need to watch your memory, Professor," Adam corrected casually as he reached across the table with his long arms to spoon more pasta onto Melchior's plate.

"I beg your pardon?" Melchior said frostily.

"More iced tea, Adam?" Verbena interrupted.

He ignored her. "Source material, Professor." Adam's eyes glinted, and Leah had the distinct impression he intended to be unpleasant. "I'm surprised that during the course of your research for your own book—which I read, by the way—you never consulted John of Sherborne."

"Who's that?" Leah asked Adam.

"He was a priest. In 1348 the Church ordered him to join a troupe of traveling players and report on their activities. Several of his original letters to the archbishop have survived and are now in the British Museum. I hope your Middle English is good, Leah. The letters have yet to be translated into modern English."

His eyes met Melchior's across the table, full of implied insult.

"Oh," Leah said, looking at her aunt for confirmation. Verbena was toying with her spaghetti.

"I have, of course, heard of those letters," Melchior said coldly, "but that subject was not the main thrust of my book. In any event, the authenticity of that source is questionable." He paused briefly before adding, "That wouldn't particularly matter to you, though, would it?"

Verbena's head snapped up. "What's for dessert, Adam?" she asked shrilly.

"And yet you quoted less reliable—though more accessible—sources in your brief mention of that period," Adam persisted.

"Coffee, anyone?" Leah interrupted. The hostility between the two men was electric. She was sorry she had initiated the discussion.

Verbena hopped out of her chair. "Coffee, yes, and dessert. Yes, that would be lovely," she babbled. "Come on, Adam, let's clear these plates. No, Leah, dear, you stay here.

We'll be just a minute." She physically propelled Adam into the kitchen.

Alone with Melchior, Leah desperately searched for a neutral topic of conversation. "So what brings you out this way, Melchior? We're a long way from Barrington."

His angry expression disappeared instantly, to be replaced by a polite social smile. Leah suspected Adam was stalking around the kitchen with a murderous scowl on his face at that moment.

"I'm lecturing for several weeks at the university as part of a special summer program. Perhaps you would like to come see me there this week to discuss your research?"

"Yes, that would be wonderful. And where are you staying while you're in town?"

"I am the guest of a colleague. Verbena offered, of course, but I'm afraid I'm not as fond of animals as she is. Where are they all, by the way?"

"All out in the backyard, except for the mynah bird."

"Thank goodness."

Adam and Verbena returned laden with a coffee tray and a beautiful lemon meringue pie that Verbena and Leah had bought in town that morning. Although he didn't look remotely apologetic, Adam nevertheless contrived to be more civil. They finished their pie in relative peace and lingered over their coffee.

"I understand there's been quite a controversy up at Mirrell University," Melchior said to Verbena.

"I haven't heard of anything."

"Nothing official has come out yet."

"In other words, it's gossip," Adam said flatly.

Melchior's eyes were as cold as a snake's when he glanced at Adam. "I think that's a rather light term to apply to what could be the end of someone's career."

"Gossip is gossip. It's only more pompous in academic circles," Adam said rudely.

"What do you mean when you say it could be the end of someone's career?" Verbena asked.

"It's quite shocking, really. There's a young man at Mirrell, a recent addition to the history department, who came to them with impeccable credentials and good recommendations. He's very popular with the students, although one might suppose that that's partially because he's very handsome. Most of his staunch supporters in this controversy are female students, after all."

"What controversy?" Adam prodded, his eyes narrowing.

Melchior patted his lips with his napkin and permitted himself a dramatic pause. "Well, it's been discovered that his credentials are phony. In point of fact, he never received his Ph.D."

"Really?" Leah asked, amazed. "And he's been teaching at an expensive private college like Mirrell?"

"Yes," Melchior confirmed. "Needless to say, it's an extreme embarrassment to the university. The chairman of the department who hired him is something of a laughingstock in the academic community at the moment." He shook his head and sighed. "It is so damaging to the image of all respectable academics when something like this gets around."

Adam snorted. "Damaging? Yes, if image is all you've got."

Leah glared at him. Her eyes moved to Verbena then. "Auntie, are you all right?"

Verbena looked pale and stunned. "That's a dreadful story, Melchior," she said huskily.

Leah glanced around the table. Adam's face darkened. Melchior practically smirked. Verbena stood and distractedly suggested they all go sit somewhere more comfortable.

"I'll clear up the table," Adam muttered. He disappeared into the kitchen with an armload of cups and plates. Leah glanced at Melchior, feeling that she should apologize for Adam's behavior, yet at the same time aware that it wasn't her place to do so.

After about a half hour of quiet, academic conversation in the front parlor, Melchior rose and said he really must be leaving. Adam still hadn't come out from the kitchen, and Leah supposed it was just as well.

As she stood in the entrance hallway with Melchior and Verbena, they heard a sudden howl of rage from the backyard. A split second later there was an enormous uproar in the kitchen.

"Macbeth! No!" Adam shouted at the back of the house. "T'ai! Chi! Come back here, dammit!"

"What the—" Leah began as King John dashed past her feet and headed toward the open front door, where Melchior was standing.

"Good Lord!" Melchior exclaimed in horror as ninety pounds of hairy, barking collie came barreling straight at him, followed by two Shih Tzus. "Arrgh!" he cried as, inevitably, Macbeth knocked him over in his rush to follow the ferret outside.

"Oh, no!" Verbena cried. T'ai and Chi jumped on top of Melchior's prostrate form. T'ai barked in his face. Chi grabbed his tie between firm jaws and made fierce little growling noises as he tugged on it.

Adam came running headlong into the entrance hallway. He stopped suddenly and took in the scene before him. Unforgivably, he burst out laughing.

"Adam, really!" Leah snapped. "Are you all right, Melchior?"

"Bad dog! Bad dog!" Verbena said, addressing T'ai and Chi individually. They ignored her.

Leah managed to prop Melchior into a sitting position. She shoved the two Shih Tzus aside. Still laughing, Adam picked up T'ai and petted him affectionately. Chi attacked one of Melchior's expensive leather shoes.

"Melchior, say something!" Verbena cried, kneeling next to him. He looked winded, dazed and disheveled.

His graying hair standing out in tufts, his tie punctured and his eyes glazed, Melchior pointed an accusing finger at Adam. "You did that on purpose!" he said hoarsely.

Still cuddling the dog, and still chuckling, Adam shook his head. "Come on, Melchior. I'm not that immature. It was an accident." He shrugged, grinning with delight. "But I couldn't have planned anything better!"

Verbena looked at him imploringly. "Adam, please!"

"Oh, all right. Relax, I'll go catch the damned ferret and get out of your way."

"Arrgh! What is *that*?" Melchior cried as another curious pet crept into the entrance hallway.

"Oh, that's the Questing Beast. Even you must have read T. H. White, Melchior. Or would admitting to that be bad for your image?" With that parting shot, Adam left the house and ran across the front lawn in search of King John and Macbeth.

Four

Verbena and Leah were shut up in the first-floor study with Archimedes, the mynah bird. Adam had a pretty good idea what they were saying.

Leah was undoubtedly saying that he was an unsuitable, disreputable, lowbrow beach boy with appalling manners. Verbena would wring her hands, since personal confrontation of that kind always upset her. She would defend his behavior today because she was fond of him. She would defend his credibility because... He didn't quite know why, actually, any more than he knew why she had proposed their partnership in the first place.

Maybe she knew she needed him.

He would have sneered at almost any other academic who had proposed collaborating with him, knowing full well why any of them might consider "lowering" themselves to his level. His books sold.

With a bunch of hypocrites. Melchior Browning epitomized all the worst aspects of academia. Verbena Mc-

Cargar, on the other hand, epitomized all that Adam had admired, all that had made him want to be a part of that exalted world of respected scholars who listed a dozen different degrees and honors after their names.

She was knowledgeable, conscientious, diligent, shrewd, demanding and a genius. She was also, however, irretrievably part of that narrow academic world that Melchior belonged to.

Adam kicked open the back door of the house with his foot and went outside. He felt tense and restless. Running after the ferret for nearly an hour had given him enough exercise, but he nevertheless couldn't sit still and concentrate. He decided to go for a walk.

That story Melchior had told them about the scandal at Mirrell had clearly shocked Verbena, he thought uncomfortably. Equally disturbing, though Adam wasn't quite sure why, was the way Leah had seemed to hang on the man's every word. Did she really buy that phony, pompous demeanor? Could someone as insubstantial as Melchior win her respect while she was busy looking down her nose at Adam?

And what gave her the right to disapprove of him so much anyhow? Adam wondered irritably. Those dark eyes, so warm when they rested on Verbena or Melchior or any of the pets, were always watchful, suspicious and critical when she looked at him.

He found an old shed toward the back of the property and wondered what it was for. A few blankets, an ancient pair of shoes and a pile of ten-year-old magazines lying inside intrigued him momentarily before he returned to pondering his problems.

His walk did nothing to improve his mood. He sauntered back toward the house, wondering how long Leah and Verbena would stay closeted in the study. He pulled some dog biscuits out of a big stoneware jar in the kitchen and fed them to Macbeth and the Shih Tzus on the back porch, feeling he should reward them for their unwitting moral support against Melchior.

The afternoon sun was warm and mellow, making him feel slightly drowsy. The hammock that was stretched out between two oak trees presented an irresistible lure. He stripped off his tank top and shoes and went to lie in it. He had had so little sleep the night before and such a trying day today that the warm sun and gentle rocking motion of the hammock soothed him into a peaceful slumber within minutes.

Leah closed the door behind her as she left the study and pressed her hands to her head, trying to ward off a headache born of frustration. Verbena hated confrontation. In this case, she was irrationally devoted to Adam and reluctant to hear any criticism about him.

Verbena had made a dozen excuses for his appalling behavior today, none of them strong enough to vindicate him in Leah's mind. Verbena had then virtually ignored every reasonable objection Leah made to Adam's credibility as a scholar and suitability as a collaborator.

She wished Mordred were here. Since he was willing to be harsher with Verbena than Leah ever was, he could sometimes make her see reason when Leah couldn't.

Mordred! Leah's head pounded anew as she remembered his phone call earlier that day. She closed her eyes in resignation. She couldn't bear to broach another difficult subject with Verbena today. It would have to wait.

She'd barely been home twenty-four hours and she was already exhausted and frustrated. She decided to go take a nap in the hammock in the backyard. It had always been her favorite spot to regain her peace of mind.

Leah went through the kitchen and out onto the back porch. Her mouth twisted when she found Macbeth and the Shih Tzus contentedly gnawing on a small pile of dog biscuits. So Adam had rewarded them, had he?

He looked like a fairy-tale prince when she found him. He was so golden in the sun he seemed to glow with radiance. His gold-tipped lashes lay on his cheeks as he slept soundly, stretched out on the hammock between two trees whose softly rustling leaves overshadowed the sound of his even breathing.

She knew he was breathing evenly, deeply, because his chest rose and fell in a steady, natural rhythm. He had taken off his shirt and shoes. Half-naked and far away in his dreams, stretched out in an attitude of abandon, he looked primitive and exotic. His muscular, hairy chest and smooth, broad shoulders emphasized all that was male about him. His legs were long and straight and leanly muscled, dusted with a fine covering of golden hair.

Her eyes traveled up his hard thighs to his narrow hips, covered by the soft, faded denim of his cutoffs. She wondered if his hair was golden everywhere....

"See anything you like?" asked a husky voice.

Leah's eyes flew up to his face. His blue eyes were open. Their expression was unfathomable.

"I . . . I thought you were asleep," she said inanely.

"Is that why you were looking at me that way?" he asked insolently.

She was instantly furious. "First you move into my room. Now you're in my hammock. What next?"

"Sorry, I didn't know it was your hammock." He didn't look at all sorry. He looked downright pleased.

"I strung it up here twelve years ago, and it's been my favorite spot ever since then," she snapped.

"And I'm defiling it?"

"You're— Never mind."

"Would you like to lie down here? There's room for both of us," he offered.

"Don't push my patience, Adam."

"You were looking at me like you had the same idea in mind," he persisted knowingly.

Leah looked away from his teasing eyes. He sat up and studied her for a long moment.

"Come on, Leah. So you find me attractive. So I find you attractive. That's not so bad, is it?"

Her brown eyes snapped with temper. "I find you presumptuous and ill-mannered."

He frowned. "And I find you tense and judgmental."

That stung, but she ignored it. "How could you be so impolite to a guest in my aunt's home?"

"Someone had to keep him in his place. You were too busy gaping at him with adolescent awe."

"I was enjoying the company of a respected scholar. And *you* have no business putting him in his place!"

"Why? Because he's got a bunch of titles and degrees? Because he's a professor?"

"Because it was unconscionably rude of you! And, yes, I think you should show respect for a man of his accomplishments."

"What accomplishments? He's a lousy teacher, a bad writer and a careless researcher."

"Why do you say that? Because his books don't make the *New York Times* Best Sellers List? Because you knew of a source that he didn't? A source, I might add, that he says is questionable."

"He was covering himself. He never heard of it. I know a lot of sources that he doesn't."

"Oh, come on, Adam."

"He's as phony as a three-dollar bill. Don't you wonder where he got that accent?"

"He—I— What does it matter?"

"He grew up in Iowa, for God's sake, and he's never spent more than a few weeks at a time in England. Don't you wonder why he talks like the Duke of York? It's an act, Leah, part of his image."

"You're out of line, Adam. Even if what you're saying is true, a man doesn't reach his position on image alone."

Adam stood and put his hands on his hips as he faced her. "So have you convinced Verbena to kick me out of the house because of today?"

Leah flushed. She should have realized he would guess why she wanted to speak privately with her aunt after Melchior's departure. She said cuttingly, "If lying around in the sun is how you earn your keep, I really can't understand why she hasn't already kicked you out."

"I do my fair share, Leah. Both on the book and around this crazy household."

She couldn't deny that he seemed to help out more than any guest should be expected to. Feeling unsettled by their angry confrontation and uncomfortable in his presence, she turned to go. "I'm going inside. Sorry to have disturbed you."

He grabbed her arm and pulled her back toward him. Her eyes flashed up to his face. "Oh, you've disturbed me all right. You're just like the rest of your breed."

She tried to pull her arm out of his grasp. "My breed? What does that mean?" she demanded.

"Academic snobs. I write books you don't need a Ph.D. to interpret, so that makes me too low to even share a dinner table with you."

"You write lurid, slushy, slick, sensationalistic—"

"What an admirable vocabulary. And which of my books have you read to make you such an authority?"

"I haven't read any of them, and I don't intend to," she said with dignity. "Now let go of me."

He didn't. He continued to stare at her. They were both breathing quickly in their anger, and the atmosphere around them seemed charged with electricity.

Leah was suddenly conscious of his nearness, his body heat, his musky scent. His chest rose and fell rapidly, drawing her gaze down to the pelt of golden hair that partially obscured two dark masculine nipples. Her heart started pounding.

Her gaze shot up to meet his, which was hooded by his lowered eyelids and his thick, gold-tipped lashes. Leah licked her lips nervously, then realized he was staring at her mouth.

"I said…let go." Her voice came out choked and husky.

Ignoring her, he kept his hold on her arm with one hand while the other came up to touch her cheek. He slowly stroked down her face and under her chin to caress the other cheek. His touch was warm and feather light.

"You're so soft," he murmured. "Like warm silk."

"Don't—"

"Why are your cheeks so hot, Leah?" he whispered. He leaned forward and let his lips replace his hand against her cheek with a soft, moist kiss. "Burning hot." He kissed her chin and then her other cheek.

Leah's chest felt as if it would burst, as if she couldn't get any air. His sexy whisper and hot touch pierced through her, setting her insides aquiver.

"Stop it." Her voice was so weak she wondered if he had even heard her. She should do something decisive, not just plead like some ninny for him to leave her alone. She should pull his hair, stomp on his foot, push him away.

When he seared her neck with another hot kiss, she felt so weak that pushing him away seemed the only alternative she had enough strength for. She brought her hands up to brace them against his chest.

The moment her hands touched him she drew in a sharp, sudden breath and forgot all about making him leave her alone. She closed her eyes, absorbed in tactile sensation. He went very still and stopped kissing her, but she could feel his warm breath against her neck as he waited for her next move.

She turned her face a little so that she could nuzzle the soft golden hair curling crisply around his head. With her blood rushing inside her ears, she moved her hands exploringly over his chest. His skin was warm and smooth and stretched tautly over iron-hard muscles. His bristly chest hair tickled her fingers, curling around them as she stroked through it in fascination.

She pulled back a little and opened her eyes to watch the play of her hands across his skin. Adam's hand stroked up her right arm and guided her palm across the hard knot of his nipple. She touched the other one without his guidance, and he shuddered suddenly, surprising them both.

Their eyes met. His were darker than she had ever seen them before. He looked questioningly at her for the space of a breath, then drew her against him. He spread his legs apart to steady his stance and draw her even closer. Ensnared between his hard thighs, with her hips pressed against his, her soft breasts rising and falling against his hard chest, her palms somehow involuntarily stroking his smooth shoulders, Leah forgot about everything in the world except this golden, pagan, fairy-tale lover and what he was doing to her.

His big hands cupped the back of her head, gripping her hair to tilt her face up to his. He lowered his mouth to hers and kissed her. There was no first-kiss awkwardness or hesitation in the firm lips that rubbed against hers or the warm, silky tongue that probed the inside of her mouth.

Her arms tightened around his neck. She met his questing tongue with her own, playing, stroking, dueling, too excited and entranced to think of anything but enjoying him and giving him pleasure in return.

Eventually they had to end the kiss to breathe, but his mouth was on hers again within the space of a heartbeat, hungrily nibbling, curiously tasting, voraciously devouring. He was so free and natural, so abandoned and demanding, she answered his hot kisses and urgent caresses with a passion she hadn't known she possessed.

She was trembling with excitement when his tongue touched hers again. She heard a low, hungry moan come from deep inside his chest and she dug her nails into his shoulders in answer. His hands slid caressingly over her back, touching her in places she had never before realized she loved to be touched. He smoothed her dress over her round bottom, then gripped the cheeks of her buttocks, pulling her closer and pushing his hips forward in a message as old as time. His tongue thrust inside her mouth with an unmistakable rhythm, echoing the demands of his hard body.

Leah cried out suddenly against his mouth, overcome by the almost painful shaft of desire that pierced through her. She started trembling, and her skin felt hot and flushed.

Adam pressed her face against his neck. He stroked her hair, her back, her bottom. He murmured words she couldn't make out.

"What?" she gasped, her hands sliding up and down his back, pressing the warm skin and tough muscles. She couldn't touch him enough.

"Not here and not in the house," he said in a strangled voice as he traced hot kisses along the side of her neck.

"What?" she repeated in breathless confusion.

"Where can we go?"

Leah went rigid as his words finally penetrated her passion-fogged brain.

"I saw a shed out back. There are a couple of blankets there," he muttered as he rubbed his cheek against her disheveled hair.

Leah raised her head and looked over his shoulder. "What?"

He tugged at her hair and tilted her face up. He grinned at her. "You keep saying that." He kissed her softly on the lips, nearly drowning her surfacing common sense.

"The shed?" she repeated between clenched teeth. He wanted to drag her off to the shed and tumble her like some witless floozy.

Summoning all her resolve, she pushed against his chest as hard as she could and backed away from him. The action threw them both off balance for a moment. She stood staring at him, shocked at herself and increasingly angry at him.

He looked unfairly gorgeous, with his golden hair rumpled from her questing hands, his blue eyes smoky with passion, his hard mouth swollen from their kisses and his beautiful body...

"Oh. My. God." Her voice was low and shaky.

"Leah?" His voice was breathless and husky.

"I don't believe this."

His eyes started to clear. He made a visible effort to control his excited breath.

Leah looked around her in dismay. How could she have let such a thing happen? He may have started it, but she wasn't hypocritical enough to pretend it was all his fault.

At last Adam said, "I'm not going to apologize, Leah."

"I don't expect you to apologize!" She couldn't deny it had been mutual.

"No, you wouldn't, would you? You figure I'm just a boorish oaf who jumps women whenever I get the chance," he snapped.

"It's pretty obvious you've had lots of practice!" A moment later she clapped a hand over her mouth in mortification. What she had just done with him was stupid enough. Did she also have to tell him how good he was at it?

Adam's face darkened. His brows swooped down in a thunderous scowl. "Verbena's probably still in the study. Why don't you run inside and tell her that in addition to all my other faults, I'm a shameless womanizer who's just attacked you?"

Her expression was equally stormy as she replied, "I do not go running to my aunt with tales of everything that goes wrong around here."

"So I've noticed. Where's Mordred?" he shot back.

All the fight went out of Leah. Embarrassment, exhaustion and a dozen different causes for worry swept over her. She took a deep breath. "That's none of your business. And I expect you to leave Mordred out of your conversations with Verbena."

He lowered his head in a gesture that signaled the end of his limited patience.

"I expect you to leave this . . . incident out of your conversations with her, too," Leah added.

His eyes flashed up to hers again, cold and angry. "This is strictly between you and me, Leah."

"This *was* strictly between us."

"Don't kid yourself that it's over. It's barely begun."

With that parting shot, he stalked back to the house in a fine cloud of rage, leaving Leah fuming by the hammock. Why did he always have to have the last word?

Adam had the unexpected good grace to make himself scarce the rest of the day. When Leah had recovered her calm enough to face Verbena at dinner, her aunt said he had gone out for the evening. She and Verbena enjoyed a quiet, peaceful evening together, catching up on old news. Feeling emotionally exhausted, Leah didn't broach any more unpleasant subjects. It was the kind of tranquil, companionable evening she had fondly imagined herself enjoying during her visit home. So why on earth, she wondered irritably, did she feel so restless and temperamental?

She tossed and turned on her well-filled but still-heaving water bed until well past midnight. Every time she started to doze, she would see Adam's smoky-blue eyes, hear his seductive whisper, feel the strength of his hands on her body and the heat of his lips on her mouth.

She sat up and punched her pillow viciously. He was right. He had started something inside her, something that was demanding to be finished. And she didn't like it. She didn't like it one little bit.

She got out of bed and paced the room in agitation. She had broken up with her last boyfriend over a year ago, and since then she had concentrated solely on her demanding studies. Adam had simply awakened dormant instincts and neglected needs, she reasoned silently. It had nothing to do with him personally, and she would simply avoid a repetition of today's embarrassing scene. Forewarned was fore-armed.

She cringed with embarrassment to think of how close she had come to pulling him down into the grass with her. She might have loathed his suggestion that they creep off to the shed like a couple of guilty teenagers, but she was honest enough to privately admit that he had shown more sense than she. They couldn't make love in the grass in full view of the house, for heaven's sake, and they certainly couldn't go up to one of their bedrooms. Verbena was liberal, certainly, but that would be going well over the limit and would put all three of them in an embarrassing position.

It shocked her to think that she had been so overheated with desire that Adam had actually been more sensitive than she to Verbena's sensibilities. She had always put Verbena and Mordred first. She couldn't think of a single instance in her life, for better or worse, when she had forgotten to consider their welfare.

"Well, it's simply not going to happen again," she said aloud in the darkened bedroom. If Adam thought otherwise, she would simply set him straight in no uncertain terms.

Satisfied that she had settled her problems to her own satisfaction, Leah crawled back into bed. Something must still be bothering her, she mused, since dawn was painting the sky pink before she began to feel even a little drowsy.

"Wake up, wake up, you sleepyhead," Verbena chirped the next morning.

Leah opened her eyes in the tiniest squint she could manage and saw Verbena standing over her bed.

"Go away," she said, groaning.

"And let you sleep the day away? You're getting to be as bad as Adam."

The mere sound of his name brought Leah to a sitting position. The bed sloshed. "What time is it?"

"Ten o'clock."

Leah groaned and squinted at the sun. She felt as if she had only had an hour or two of sleep, which wasn't far off the mark, she decided grumpily. Damn Adam!

She tumbled out of bed, then washed, dressed and went downstairs, hoping there was still some coffee left. Adam was sitting at the kitchen table with a bland, sleepy expression on his face as he listened to Verbena chatter away.

"I've made some fresh coffee, dear. I had mine hours ago," Verbena said cheerfully as she filled Leah's cup and refilled Adam's.

"Good morning," Leah said crisply to Adam.

"Mmmph," he replied. He yawned.

They both listened to Verbena recount the antics of the iguana that morning. By the time he had finished his second cup of coffee, Adam seemed to be entering the world of the living. His eyes opened wide as he studied Leah.

"You don't look as perfect as usual," he said candidly.

She glared at him.

"She didn't sleep well last night." Verbena clucked worriedly and fussed over Leah, trying to make her eat her toast.

"Really, I'm not hungry, Auntie. I'll wait till lunch."

"You didn't sleep well?" Adam asked. He looked positively alert now, Leah noticed irritably. And unforgivably cocky.

"No," she said stonily.

"I wonder why?" His tone was insufferably innocent.

"She's overwrought from such a difficult year at the university," Verbena said matter-of-factly.

"Funny. I couldn't sleep last night, either." Adam paused before asking softly, "Do you suppose there's a connection?"

"No," Leah answered tersely. She rose abruptly. "Didn't you say you wanted to go shopping today, Auntie?"

"Yes, dear, I do. Do you want to come along, Adam?"

"No, thanks. I've got work to do," he replied.

"But you might—"

"Nonsense, Auntie. If he's going to work instead of lie around in the sun or terrorize your guests, don't talk him out of it." Leah propelled Verbena out of the room, glad to have the last word with Adam for once. He spoiled the victory, however, by laughing.

She avoided Adam as much as possible the rest of the week and concentrated on enjoying Verbena's company and sorting out her aunt's domestic life. Verbena took her shopping again, insisting she hadn't brought enough clothes with her. With characteristic generosity, Verbena bought her enough clothes to last well into the following summer.

Leah spent an entire day figuring out which bills had to be paid and which legal letters had to be answered. Then she cornered Verbena and forced her to write the necessary checks and sign the necessary letters. Workmen tromped around all week, repairing the neglected house as Leah directed.

Mordred's next phone call came toward the end of the week. Adam answered the call and handed Leah the receiver. When she realized it was Mordred, she waited for Adam to leave the room before continuing the conversation.

"Where are you?" she whispered. "I'm running out of excuses for Verbena."

"I can't tell you where I am," was the response.

She gripped the receiver in agitation. "Are you in trouble?"

"Do not concern yourself about me, Leah," he said in a gooey, nobler-than-thou tone.

Leah pulled away to stare at the receiver in disbelief for a moment. She blinked, then asked, "When are you coming home?"

"I'm afraid I'm not, cousin."

"We agreed—"

"I know, but I regret that I can't make it."

She frowned. His voice was peculiar, stilted and unnatural. "What's going on? Mordred, for God's sake—"

"I'm going to Bolivia!" he cried suddenly. "That's Bolivia, I say!"

"Bolivia?"

"I'm afraid it's the only solution. Don't look for me again, Leah. Tell anyone who asks not to look for me. This is goodbye forever, my dear."

"But you don't know anyone in Bolivia. You don't even speak Spanish."

"It's too late."

"For what?"

"Remember me to Mother."

"Mordred!" she shouted into the receiver. He had hung up.

She put the receiver back in its cradle. The whole tone of that conversation, right down to his melodramatic announcement that he was going to Bolivia—"it's the only solution"—was totally unlike her capricious cousin. What on earth was he doing? she wondered. If this was some sort of silly prank, she would shred all his Pierre Cardin sweaters when she finally got her hands on him.

If he was actually in some kind of trouble...

Leah took a deep breath and squared her shoulders. She would, in any event, have to tell Verbena that Mordred wasn't coming home. Cursing her thoughtless cousin under her breath, she went into the study where Adam and Verbena were working.

She broke it as gently as she could and offered minimal explanations, wanting to shield Verbena without fabricating deliberate lies. Adam looked at her broodingly as she made her speech. She wasn't sure if he believed her or not. Perhaps he was just brooding because of the careful, conscientious way she had avoided him all week.

Verbena was obviously hurt. Her dark eyes misted over. She excused herself, saying she would take a walk and feed the raccoons. Adam blocked Leah's way as she tried to follow her aunt out of the room.

"Does he know how much she was looking forward to this?" Adam challenged.

Torn between her anger at Mordred for hurting Verbena and her loyalty to him against an outsider, Leah shrugged uncomfortably.

Adam looked at her shrewdly. "Is there more to this than you're telling her?"

"What do you mean?" she asked weakly.

"What's really going on with that kid?"

"He's a full-grown man. And how dare you criticize him? I notice you're not visiting your mother right now."

"But I do visit her more than once every two years, and I don't promise to show up and then back out," he shot back.

"This is a family matter and none of your business!" she snapped, pushing her way past him.

"Wait." He put a hand on her shoulder, gently but firmly restraining her. He took a deep breath and lowered his head. Finally he said, "You're right for once. It *is* none of my business, and I'm sorry for butting in. I'm just…concerned about Verbena."

His humble apology and his honest concern for her aunt reached out to her. She felt a warmth toward him quite out of proportion to the circumstances. "I—I guess I over-reacted, too. I appreciate your concern for Verbena. But I know Mordred and you don't, and I can assure you that our arguing about him won't change matters."

He nodded. His eyes searched her face. "And we've already got enough to argue about, haven't we?" His voice was soft.

"We…" She lowered her eyes. He touched a finger to her chin, gently forcing her to meet his gaze again.

"What would it take," he murmured musingly, "to make you as loyal to me as you are to Mordred and Verbena?"

She stared at him, feeling vulnerable and tender. "I don't know," she whispered helplessly.

"If you figure it out, I hope you let me know."

He leaned forward and brushed a soft, feather-light kiss on her mouth. She kept her eyes closed as she felt him walk by her. She pressed a hand to her mouth as if to seal their kiss as she heard him saunter down the hall toward the kitchen.

Five

————

Where's Adam?'' Leah demanded the next afternoon as she stalked into the kitchen.

''You look very pretty. Did you have a nice meeting with Melchior, dear?''

''Yes. A very interesting meeting, in fact.''

''He's a useful contact,'' Verbena said as she chopped up papaya for the Questing Beast.

''In more ways than one. Where's Adam?''

''In the study, I think? Why?''

''I need to talk to him.'' She started out of the room and then stopped abruptly and asked, ''Where will *you* be?''

Her aunt looked at her peculiarly. ''I don't know, dear. In here, I suppose.''

''Good,'' Leah said. She shifted awkwardly, then repeated, ''Good.''

She walked rapidly down the hallway, through the dining room, past the entrance hall and into the study.

He was there all right. He lay napping on the couch with a book over his face. Loafing as usual, Leah thought disgustedly. She pulled the book away from his face and read the title: *Norman Influence on Anglo-Saxon Socio-Sexual Relationships*.

Leah sneered. After what she had just learned, she doubted he could even understand that book. The golden boy was quite an actor. He had fooled everyone into believing he was a historian.

Adam opened his eyes and peered up at her. "Do you need that book, Leah?" he asked casually.

"No. And I don't think you'll be needing it, either."

He ran a hand over his face. "I wish I didn't. Tedious stuff."

"Perhaps it's a little above you," she said disdainfully.

He looked at her warily. There was no mistaking her tone for light jest.

"But no matter," she continued. "If what I've heard is true, I doubt you'll be spending another night in this house. Or working another day on Verbena's book."

He sat up and scowled at her. "It's *our* book. And what have you heard that's so earthshaking?"

"I met with Melchior Browning today."

That got his attention. He swung his legs over the edge of the couch and stood. He put his hands on his hips. His whole body appeared tense, as if ready for an attack. "Go on."

"He told me a rather shocking story. One that I'm sure Verbena doesn't know."

"Really?" His tone was as dry as a desert wind.

She met his gaze levelly, not bothering to hide her anger. "According to Professor Browning, you never got your Ph.D. In fact, you were kicked out of the program."

"I wasn't kicked out. I quit," he flared.

"Oh, well, that makes *all* the difference," Leah said with heavy sarcasm. "Never mind that you've led the whole world—including *my aunt*—to believe that, despite your dubious reputation and even more dubious books, you at least possessed a doctorate from a respected university. I'm sure everyone, if they knew the truth, would simply agree that quitting a doctoral program is somehow different from being thrown out of one, and therefore entitles you to call yourself a doctor!"

"I don't call myself a doctor."

"In this very house, you told Melchior to call you *Dr. Jordan*," she reminded him.

"So Melchior, that slime bucket, invited you for a chat and, as soon as you walked through the door, said, 'Leah, my dear, I must warn you that your aunt's partner is a fraud'?"

"No."

"No? Then how did he worm it into the conversation?"

"Does it matter?"

"It does to me. More than you can guess."

Leah folded and unfolded her hands, suddenly feeling defensive. "We were talking about my dissertation, and since you had been a doctoral candidate in his department, I naturally asked him about your dissertation."

"You did?" He forgot his anger for a moment in his surprise. Then his face darkened. "You mean you asked him if it was any good, don't you?"

"I wouldn't be that indiscreet," she replied uncomfortably.

"But that was the general idea, wasn't it?"

"Don't try to turn this conversation around! Imagine my surprise when I learned that your dissertation was so bad that Professor Browning advised you to start over from scratch and spend another year at Barrington. And that you refused to."

"Did he tell you that, as my adviser and as chairman of the department, he refused to let me present and defend my dissertation? That he thought his narrow-minded, uninspired, unenlightened judgment was important enough to squelch my academic career?"

"Adam," she said in exasperation, "that's what advisers and department heads are for!"

"He tried to use his position to mandate what I could say about history, and how I could say it," Adam said accusingly.

"If I make ridiculous or irresponsible deductions in my thesis, then it's my adviser's responsibility to warn me against presenting it, and it's the department head's duty to make sure I don't go spreading my irresponsible message with a degree from his university standing next to my name."

"He told you I made irresponsible and ridiculous deductions?" Adam demanded.

She drew a deep breath. "Well . . . not exactly."

They stared at each other for a long moment. Finally Adam said wearily, "And as mediocre and pretentious as he is, you still believed him wholeheartedly because you're so contemptuous of my career, is that it?"

The bitterness in his voice pierced through her, making her absurdly sorry she had brought up the whole subject. But she must get to the heart of the matter for Verbena's sake. "Then it's true, isn't it?"

"That I was kicked out? I already told you it isn't. I quit while he was trying to get me kicked out."

"But you didn't get your Ph.D. then, did you?"

"That's what Melchior said?"

"Yes."

"And that's all he said?"

"Yes."

He released his breath on a puff of air that sufficed as a bitter laugh.

Leah smoothed the folds of her new linen dress. "What you do in your own career is no concern of mine. But how could you collaborate with my aunt and risk making her the laughingstock of the entire academic community? What kind of a person are you?"

He turned away from her to look out the window. "You've already decided what kind of person I am. Why bother asking?"

"How could you do this to her?"

He glanced over his shoulder at her. "Are you even interested in hearing my side of the story?"

"Frankly, no. All I'm interested in right now is protecting Verbena. You've got to tell her the truth, Adam. Whether you quit or were thrown out, you're not a qualified scholar, and she has the right to know. You've got to tell her."

He leaned an arm against the window frame and rested his forehead against it. He took a deep breath.

The phone rang. The noise was so piercing in the silent tension of the room that Leah nearly jumped out of her skin. It rang twice and then stopped. Verbena must have answered it in the kitchen.

"Adam . . ." Leah prodded.

He straightened away from the window. "You're right, of course. It's absolutely the only thing you're right about, but, yes, I have to tell Verbena. Immediately."

"She's very mild tempered. I'm sure she won't castigate you," Leah said, wondering why on earth she felt like she should be comforting him.

He almost looked amused. "I'm not afraid of Verbena, Leah. I'm not even afraid of you."

"Very funny."

"But I will be sorry for both Verbena and myself if we don't get to write this book together."

Leah chose not to comment, since she was certain that the very best thing that could happen to Verbena would be to lose Adam's assistance in this endeavor.

"Come on, let's do it now," he said restlessly. "You'll no doubt want to listen to make sure I don't try to absolve myself in any way."

"Don't you dare try to make me the villain of this piece," Leah answered defensively. "You're the one who's been hiding the truth from my aunt. And Melchior's the one who spilled the beans. I just seem to be the only person around here who has considered how this could affect Verbena.''

"Isn't she lucky that you came home to protect her from me, then?''

Leah glared at Adam's back as he left the room before her. Once again, she realized, he had contrived to have the last word.

Verbena was on the telephone when they entered the kitchen, apparently finishing the conversation.

As soon as she hung up, Adam said, "Verbena, there's something I have to tell you.''

"Can it wait?'' Verbena asked, her gaze focused on the telephone.

"It's very important, Auntie,'' Leah added.

Verbena stepped back and slumped into a chair. She raised her face to them. It was pale and tense.

"Auntie!'' Leah gasped. "What's wrong?''

"That phone call . . .''

"Yes?'' Leah said.

"It was from England.''

"Yes?''

"It was Grimly's sister.''

Leah swallowed. Adam looked back and forth from one woman to the other.

"Is Grimly all right?'' Leah asked.

"He's going into the hospital next week for surgery. They're afraid it might be . . . something very serious.''

"Oh, Auntie.'' Leah went to her aunt and put her arms around her.

Feeling confused but aware that this was no time to ask questions, Adam sat down at the table, too.

After a few moments of silence, Verbena pulled away from Leah. "Well, I really must pack,'' she said.

"Pack?'' said Leah.

"Pack?'' said Adam.

"Of course. I've got to be there.''

Adam's eyes met Leah's. He could see that she couldn't decide what to say.

"Leah, will you please call the airline and make arrangements? I want to leave right away. This evening, if possible."

"I—"

"Thank you, dear." Verbena stood and left the room swiftly, leaving them both staring after her in bemusement.

"Who's Grimly?" Adam asked at last.

Leah slumped into the same chair Verbena had slumped into. "Grimly Corridor, the famous anthropologist."

"Grimly Corridor? You've got to be kidding." She frowned at him. He shrugged. "Sorry. Is he close to your family?"

She hesitated before answering. "He's Mordred's father."

"What?"

Leah nodded.

"How?"

She frowned at him again.

"I mean, I know *how*, but . . ." He spread his hands in a gesture of confusion. "You know what I mean."

Leah sighed. "It's a long story. He and Verbena met nearly forty years ago. He was a student at Cambridge. Verbena had been awarded a special scholarship to study there for a year. They fell in love."

"Wow." Adam tried to picture Verbena all those years ago.

"They got engaged and nearly went through with the wedding."

"What went wrong?"

"A lot of things. He's moody and intractable." She chuckled as she added, "And he hates animals."

"Ahh."

"But mostly, he wanted to spend the rest of his life studying the few remaining stone-age cultures in existence, and Verbena wanted to be a historian. She didn't see a future for herself in Amazonian jungles. So she broke off the engagement and came back to America.''

Adam frowned. ''So how did Mordred happen?''

''Years later, when Verbena was in her late thirties, she was at a conference in Paris at the same time Grimly was there reporting his findings to some institute.''

''And they found the old chemistry was still there between them?''

''Yes. And Mordred was the result.''

''Did Grimly want to marry her?''

''Well, by the time Verbena realized Mordred was on the way, Grimly was back in his jungle, incommunicado. So she had Mordred and went about raising him. Mordred was about five years old before Grimly and Verbena got in touch again.''

''What happened then?''

''Everyone's always been a little vague about that. I gather Mordred and Grimly didn't get along particularly well. Verbena said it was apparent within days that the three of them could never make a family together.''

''So Grimly went back off to his jungle and Verbena raised Mordred alone.''

''Yes. It wasn't always easy on either of them, but I've met Grimly and, well, he's a remarkable man, but I wouldn't want to have to live in the same house with him, either.''

''Did Mordred ever see him again?''

''Just a few times.'' She grinned. ''They still don't like each other much. Even so, Grimly is the great love of Verbena's life. He surfaces every few years. I'm not surprised she wants to be with him.''

''In that case, maybe you'd better call the airline and get her on a plane to England.''

''Yes, of course.''

The next few hours were so hectic Leah forgot about everything except the emergency at hand. Verbena, despite years of travel, had an imperfect understanding of packing and wound up asking Leah to help her. Then they had to take notes while she dictated a series of complicated instructions about feeding, cleaning and caring for the menagerie and the local wildlife. As soon as they were done with that, she realized they would also need a list of appointments and obligations that had to be postponed while she was away.

Short on time, they drove her to the local airport for her connecting flight to JFK while she continued scribbling down important phone numbers and addresses.

Just before boarding the plane, Verbena turned to Adam and said, "Oh, my goodness! We haven't even discussed what to do next on the book!"

"I know what to do next, Verbena. Don't worry, I'll handle it," he said calmly.

"You'll be sure to verify the sources we talked about yesterday?"

Adam nodded and reassured her.

"Auntie, they're announcing last call for your flight."

"Oh, dear, I hate flying!"

"Did you bring something to read?"

"Yes."

"Where's your boarding pass?"

"Right here."

"Call us when you arrive. Give my regards to Grimly."

"I will, dear." Verbena hugged her. Tears misted in her eyes. "I had so looked forward to your coming home, and now here I am leaving you."

"It couldn't be helped, Auntie. And when Grimly's better, you'll come back and I'll still be here."

"Yes, of course. Adam." She hugged him and kissed his cheek. "Try to get more rest, and don't let anybody imply that you're not—"

"Auntie, the stewardess doesn't look like she'll wait any longer."

Adam planted a kiss on Verbena's pale cheek. "Have a safe trip. And bring us back something good."

Leah drove home in silence, wrestling with her thoughts. Adam was equally quiet, staring out the window and letting the breeze caress his face.

She pulled into the driveway, brought the car to a halt and turned off the engine. The silence between them was suddenly deafening.

"Are you really going to keep working on the book?" Leah asked at last.

"Yes. She wants me to."

"She doesn't know the truth."

"Are you so positive that she'll throw me out on my ear once I tell her?"

Leah shrugged and stared out into the darkness. Verbena's fondness for Adam might cloud her judgment. Quite apart from his subterfuge about his degree, Leah had considered him a poor choice on her aunt's part from the start. She got out of the car and walked toward the house, aware of Adam following behind her.

She opened the front door and went inside. Behind her, Adam slammed it shut. She whirled in surprise.

"That got your attention," he said dryly.

"Was that the purpose?"

"Yes." He stalked forward and stood close before her. "I'm actually a pretty even-tempered guy, Leah, but you would test the patience of a saint at times."

"I think we can both agree that you're no saint."

"Exactly. And for the sake of domestic harmony while Verbena's away, I think we ought to get a few things straight."

"Such as?"

"You've criticized my previous books without having read them, and you've castigated me for my past at Barrington University while refusing to hear my side of the story. I realize you think you're acting in Verbena's best interests. But whatever you may think of me personally or professionally, I swear to you I would never do anything to hurt Verbena. In fact, I doubt if anyone else would be will-

ing to accept taking care of her house and her beasts as part
of their obligation to her as a collaborator.''

He had a point, though Leah was reluctant to say so.

Both their heads jerked around as they heard a sudden
howl of rage from the backyard. Macbeth and King John
were at it again. The iguana came skittering past them and
ran into the study. Within moments the mynah bird flew out
of the study and down the hallway, cursing viciously in
Middle English.

"Good Lord," Adam said.

"Very well, Adam. Considering our present situation, I
suggest we call a truce and join forces."

He nodded. A familiar grin split his face. "Okay. You go
catch the mynah bird before he stains something. I'll go pull
apart the collie and the damned ferret."

Six

Their truce was short-lived.

"What is this?" Leah demanded angrily as she confronted Adam on the back porch the next afternoon. She waved a crumpled piece of paper under his nose.

He dropped the fifty-pound bag of cracked corn he had been carrying and tore the paper out of her hands.

"I've been looking everywhere for this!" he exclaimed. Without warning, he grabbed her and planted a kiss on her cheek. "Thank you, Leah! Where'd you find it?"

Sputtering with fury she backed away from him. "I found it in T'ai's mouth."

Adam leveled a menacing glare on T'ai, who had followed Leah outside. The Shih Tzu returned his look innocently. "Bad dog," Adam said without conviction. "You're lucky you're so cute."

"And since *you* are not ten pounds, four-legged and covered with fur, I want an explanation," Leah said, annoyed that Adam didn't have the good grace to look sheepish or ashamed.

"*I* don't know how he got it. I'll try to keep paper away from him in the future, but—"

"That's not what I'm talking about," Leah snapped.

"Then what?"

She grabbed the letter back from him. Unconcerned, he stooped to pick up the bag of cracked corn and carried it down to the large feed bins Verbena kept next to the porch.

Leah read aloud, "'Dear Adam, I loved the first few chapters of *A Viable Alternative* (and agree with you that *Licentious Nuns* would make a better title if you can get your collaborator to agree to it).'"

She cast him a scathing glance before continuing. "'I look forward to discussing a contract for this book when you come to the city later this month.' And so on and so forth."

Having poured all the cracked corn into the feed bin, Adam straightened up to look at Leah. "So?"

"It's from Lavish Books!"

"Of course it is," he said reasonably, turning to fill a hand scoop with cracked corn.

"Is that all you have to say?" Leah demanded incredulously.

"Calm down, Leah, you look like you might hyperventilate at any moment," Adam chided. He rounded the house with his scoop of corn.

Fuming with rage, Leah trailed behind him. She had expected denials and excuses, but not this casual unconcern. He was filling a bird feeder when she caught up with him.

"Do we put cracked corn or sunflower seeds in this one?" he asked, frowning at the empty feeder.

"How the devil should I know?"

He raised his brows. "*You* took the notes last night when Verbena was spewing out all that information."

"Bird food is bird food! Can't we talk about something more important?"

"Like what?"

"Like the way you're prostituting my aunt's work to some slick, mainstream, lowbrow, uncultured publisher!"

"That's *my* publisher, Leah."

"Precisely!"

He grimaced, shrugged off the insult, filled the bird feeder and walked past her to the back of the house again.

"Give me patience," Leah said to the blue summer sky.

"If we put cracked corn in this one, where do we put the sunflower seeds?" Adam asked when she approached him again.

"Does Verbena know?"

"I should think so, they're her birds. But if you've lost the instructions—"

"I mean, does she know about Lavish Books?" Leah clarified between clenched teeth.

"Not yet. I meant to tell her yesterday, but so much happened that I plumb forgot about it."

"Adam, this is outrageous!"

He put his hands on his hips and turned to face her, abandoning his casual manner. He was clearly getting annoyed. "Leah, the book has to be published. I'm certainly not going to sign anything without Verbena's permission, but it's a good idea to start stirring up interest. Now that we've got a few chapters ready, we'd like to get a contract."

"But with a responsible publisher."

"They *are* responsible. I've done four books for them, gotten paid well and benefited from excellent publicity and good distribution. Verbena's checking out her contacts, I'm checking out mine. We'll make the decision—*together*— when we decide who is making the most desirable offer."

"She'll never agree to sign with a publisher like that."

"Like what? You make them sound like underground pornographers."

"They're fine for spy novels and movie-star biographies, but Verbena writes serious scholarly studies."

"She knew they were my publishers when she first approached me," he reminded her. "She knew they were a possible market for *our* book. May I suggest that you're overreacting to this?"

He picked up a scoopful of sunflower seeds and went in search of a bird feeder. Leah sat down on the porch steps. By the time he returned, she had calmed down enough to approach him from a different angle.

"Considering that we have yet to tell Verbena that you were thrown out of—sorry, *quit*—your doctoral program, and considering that she may well call an end to your association when you do tell her, don't you think you're being a bit premature?"

"In trying to sell the book, you mean?"

She nodded.

He shrugged, his good mood restored after his brief outburst. "No. If she doesn't drop me like a hot rock, it's time well spent. And if she does spurn me, which I just know you're counting on, Miss McCargar, then consider the groundwork my gift to her. For all you know, she may decide to sell the book to a lucrative market even without me."

Leah's expression told him what she thought of that assertion.

"Now while you have been castigating me for something that's not really any of your business—" he began.

"Somebody's got to—"

"I know. Somebody's got to look after poor, silly, helpless Aunt Verbena who's just too naive to make any decisions on her own."

Leah's eyes widened and she was speechless with surprise for a moment. She was stung by the scathing tone of his voice. And his words were entirely inappropriate. "I . . . I never—" she stammered, not even sure what she wanted to say in response.

He tilted his head. "Oh, no?"

"She's the most brilliant woman alive. I have nothing but respect and admiration for her. She relies on me to...to..."

"So I've noticed," he said dryly. "But what I can't figure out is why a healthy young woman like you, with a busy life of your own, is still so overprotective of her. You moved out when you were eighteen?"

"Yes."

"And she's still alive and well and lauded in her field. Did it ever occur to you that she doesn't need you to protect her quite so fiercely?"

Leah was quiet for a long moment, resisting the urge to squirm under his piercing regard.

Finally Adam broke the silence. "Well, maybe it's none of my business."

Leah looked at her feet. She didn't know why she suddenly felt like crying. It was absurd, of course, to even suppose that Verbena didn't need her. She was surprised that she didn't feel more resentful toward Adam for suggesting it, or for speculating about her family relationships. Instead, she just wanted to stop fighting with him.

"Need help with the feeding?" she asked softly, hoping to change the subject.

He grinned. He was always willing to end a fight, Leah acknowledged gratefully.

"Absolutely. You didn't think I'd let you get away with making me do it all alone, did you?"

"What's left?"

"The raccoons."

She smiled ruefully. Their feeding spot was a long way from the house.

"Just to reestablish our truce, I'll walk down with you, okay?" he offered.

"Okay," she agreed, realizing she would be glad for his company.

"Why does Verbena feed them so far from the house, anyhow?"

Leah realized that Adam's usual cheerful demeanor was already lightening her mood. "Verbena used to feed them right off the back porch. Then came the summer that

Grimly stopped in for a visit. He was only here for five days, but his presence disrupted our normal routine so much that one day Verbena simply forgot to feed the raccoons.''

"Verbena forgot to feed an animal? That must have been a memorable visit.''

"I told you Grimly isn't the sort of person you'd want to live with full-time. Anyhow, when the raccoons came up for their evening meal and found it wasn't there, they simply lost all sense of proportion. They raided all the feed bins, tore up the garden, shredded the screen on the back door and then attacked Mordred when he came out to investigate the commotion.''

Adam chuckled. "Poor Mordred. No wonder he hates animals. He always gets the short end of the stick in your stories.''

They fed the raccoons, and Leah shared more lurid stories about growing up in Verbena's house as they walked back. When they returned to the house, they received a phone call from Verbena telling them she had arrived safely and was staying in a hotel in London.

They shared a simple meal of soup and sandwiches, each separately choosing to steer clear of any topic that might arouse further conflict between them. They had enough on their hands at the moment.

After they ate, Adam retired to his room to work on the book, and Leah went to the study to do the first work on her thesis she had even attempted since arriving a week earlier. She didn't see Adam the rest of the night, which was probably just as well. As soon as their animosity had subsided, a disturbing sexual tension had resurfaced between them.

It was one thing to avoid being alone with him when Verbena was around, but now the two of them were alone in the house with no chaperone. Leah had always loved this house, but suddenly it was affecting her in a new and unfamiliar way.

All day long the sun shone through the windows, casting rays of light that changed in color and intensity as morning turned to afternoon and evening turned to twilight. Adam looked special in every shade and shadow of light: fresh and golden in the morning, bronzed and glorious at noon, warm and mysterious in the darkening glow of a summer evening.

Soft breezes coursed through the house day and night from two dozen open windows, carrying the scent of wildflowers and freshly mowed fields. It brushed Leah's skin with a feather-light touch that made her think of Adam's caress so often she couldn't meet his eyes without feeling her pulse race.

As she lay in her sweetly scented, darkened bedroom with her hair strewn over the pillows that night, she watched the moon glow reflect off the clouds and paint a celestial pageant in the sky.

It would be so easy to slip out the door and go to Adam's room, she reflected drowsily. Just a few steps and a simple knock. He would know instantly why she had come. He wouldn't even make her explain. He would just enfold her in his warm arms, draw her against his hard chest, lower his firm lips to hers and . . .

She rolled over on her side and hugged her pillow, resigning herself to another restless night, courtesy of Adam Jordan.

A few rooms down the hall, Adam stared at the ceiling and wondered what Leah would look like in a bed flooded by moonlight. Her skin would be as pale as alabaster, and her thick, dark hair would look nearly black. Those big, serious eyes would gleam with little flecks of moon glow as she looked at him. She would open her arms to him, and sink to the mattress with him, pliant and soft, warm and giving.

"More likely she'd stab me with a letter opener. Or talk me to death," he muttered.

He rolled onto his stomach and wished he could stop thinking about her. She had no respect for him and probably never would. She thought he was a fraud, and even the truth probably wouldn't change her mind. She had said only the night before that she didn't even want to hear his side of the story. She just wanted to keep him from besmirching her family name.

He rolled back onto his back and put his arms behind his head. It had been hard enough to keep his hands off her when Verbena was around. This evening had been sheer torture. He had gone directly to his room after dinner to avoid making a fool of himself. Despite her unexpected passionate response to him a few days ago, Leah had made a point of letting him know that she wouldn't welcome his advances. He had never been shy with women, even with seemingly unapproachable ones, but he also wasn't some kind of macho creep who forced his attentions on a woman.

If Leah wasn't interested in him, that was her prerogative and he would just have to keep his longing to himself. If she thought he was beneath her—which she obviously did—then that was her loss and just too damned bad.

He shifted restlessly, feeling hurt anew by her attitude. He had caught her looking at him a few times, much in the same way he couldn't help looking at her. Why couldn't she just give in and enjoy him for himself? Why did he have to possess a Ph.D. and publish dry, dusty, scholarly tomes that no one but a historian could appreciate in order to win Leah's favor?

She actively resisted the attraction between them—and for such superficial, pretentious, insubstantial, snobbish reasons, it made him want to shake her till her teeth rattled.

He had briefly considered going away and not coming back until Verbena returned. He couldn't. He couldn't leave Leah alone with the house and the menagerie, that would be too selfish. And he couldn't just leave the book at a standstill. Whatever Verbena decided when he broke the news to her, he felt honor bound to continue working until then.

Besides, if he were honest, he didn't want to leave. Despite everything, he'd rather stay with Leah. He ruefully wondered when he had developed this penchant for self-torture.

The next morning, Leah acknowledged that the enormous task of cleaning Verbena's house was too daunting for her to contemplate alone. It would take half the summer, and despite his willingness to share the burden in all other matters, Adam refused to help clean the house.

"I was thinking we should start with your room," Leah said acidly after he had said the house looked all right to him.

"Don't you touch it. I'd never find anything again."

"How can you work in that mess?"

"The mess is a good sign. It means I'm too busy to tidy up. A *clean* workroom is a sign that I can't concentrate."

"In any event, the rest of the house is covered with dust, dead leaves, animal hair and food crumbs."

"Maybe it could use a good once-over," Adam conceded.

She looked at him hopefully.

"No," he said stubbornly. "I'm already busy feeding half the animals in western New York."

Since he clearly couldn't be persuaded in this matter, and since she didn't really want to do it, either, Leah contacted Jenny Harper that very morning. Jenny, Verbena's former cleaning woman—and the only cleaning woman in Ithaca who liked the menagerie—came over for coffee that afternoon.

"He seems quite horrible at first, but he's rather endearing once you get to know him," Leah was saying when Adam sauntered into the kitchen.

"Talking about me?" he asked.

"No, the Questing Beast," Leah answered. "Adam, this is Jenny Harper."

Jenny was about thirty and usually madly in love with her husband, but Leah noticed that Adam's appearance made her preen and flirt like a debutante. He responded with friendly jokes and smiles. Leah was suddenly conscious of

an unexpected and unpleasant emotion that she had no right
to feel and which did her character no credit at all.

"I'm sorry Verbena hasn't been able to get anyone else to
work for her," Jenny said. "It's a shame other folks don't
like her cute little pets."

She cooed and clucked over King John when he came
slinking into the room. Leah and Adam exchanged a determined glance. They had to hire this woman back, no matter what it took.

Once they got down to bargaining, Leah found Jenny's
request unusual, but easy to accommodate.

"You want to exorcise the ghost?" Adam said incredulously.

"Yes. You let me do that, and I'll be happy to come back
to work here."

Leah wrapped her hands around her coffee mug. "Jenny,
I don't want to impugn your veracity—"

"Come again?" Jenny said.

"She doesn't want to call you a liar," Adam said, casting Leah an exasperated look.

"But I grew up in this house, and I never once noticed
anything unusual here." Adam laughed at that. "I mean a
spiritual presence," she amended wryly.

"It's there, Leah," Jenny assured her. "You and your
family aren't sensitive to it, but I feel it all the time I'm here.
A hostile, angry presence, reaching out and ruining my se-
renity."

Adam and Leah exchanged another glance. "Well," Leah
said at last, "by all means, let's exorcise it, then. And you'll
start work as soon as it's gone?"

"Sure. This place is a mess, if you'll excuse me saying so."

"We'll excuse it," Adam assured her. "Uh, how long will
this exorcism take?"

"That depends on how much the intruder wants to stay
here."

"I see," said Leah, not seeing at all.

"How do we get started?" Adam asked.

"We'll need to measure the dimensions of its power center first of all," Jenny explained. "Have you got a tape measure?"

Exorcising a ghost with a tape measure sounded a little prosaic to Leah, but she fetched one anyhow. Then she and Adam followed Jenny up to the third floor of the house.

"It's stuffy up here," Adam observed.

"No one ever uses these rooms. Verbena just keeps junk stored up here," Leah explained.

"In that room," Jenny said, pointing to a door at the end of the hall.

There was a faded word painted across the top of the door.

"Xanadu?" Adam read aloud. He glanced sharply at Leah and then grinned. "Don't tell me that's where Kubla Khan, the notorious python, lived?"

Leah nodded. "Mordred painted that sign years ago. I don't think I've come up here since I got rid of the snake."

"Maybe he's the hostile presence she senses," Adam said as Jenny disappeared into the room.

"Don't be silly. Kubla Khan is still alive and well. No doubt he's terrorizing some hapless zookeeper at this very moment."

Jenny measured the room, whirled around a few times and made some alarming moaning noises. After ten minutes they all went back downstairs. Jenny told them she would be back with an expert.

The following morning, a new problem arose.

"There's a lizard in the bathtub," Adam said.

Leah glanced up from her coffee cup and newspaper. Adam had clearly just gotten out of bed. He looked disheveled and cuddly and adorable, all rugged six feet of him. Since he was always incoherent in the morning, she simply poured him a cup of coffee and went back to reading her paper, ignoring his comment.

"Did you hear me?" he persisted. "There's a lizard in the bathtub."

"Of course there is," she said soothingly and pushed his coffee toward him.

He sat down at the kitchen table and stared at her for a full minute. She finally looked up at him. He was clearly trying to marshal his thoughts.

"I went into the bathroom to take a shower. And I turned on the water."

There was a long silence. He seemed to have lost his train of thought.

"Go on," she said encouragingly. "You turned on the water."

"Where?"

"In the tub."

"Oh, yeah." That got him back on track. "And I turned on the shower spray and stepped under it."

"And?"

"And I was attacked by a lizard."

She stared at him.

"I swear it on my honor."

She raised her brows dubiously.

"If you don't believe me, come see for yourself."

"All right," she said resignedly.

He had probably stepped on one of the rubber bath toys that Verbena had an inexplicable fondness for, and in his groggy condition he had mistaken it for a real menace. She followed him upstairs and preceded him into the bathroom. Under his bleary but watchful gaze, she pulled aside the shower curtain and looked into the tub.

A nasty reptile hissed at her.

She pulled Adam out of the bathroom and slammed the door shut in less than three seconds.

"There's a lizard in the bathtub," she said.

"Hah! So you admit it."

"How on earth did it get there?"

"I know the plumbing in this house is old, but *really*," Adam said in amazement.

"Go have some coffee. You're useless to me in this condition," she chided.

He did as he was told. While he was trying to wake up, Leah braved another peek at the lizard. Adam was looking relatively alert by the time he came back upstairs to find her sitting in the hallway puzzling out their problem.

"It's one of Verbena's lizards," she told him as he sat down on the floor next to her.

"She keeps lizards, too? Doesn't she draw the line anywhere?" he demanded.

"It's not quite like that. Last time I was home, we were having a terrible problem with insects and Verbena was spending a fortune on pesticides and fumigation. It was inconvenient for us and dangerous to the animals."

"What does this have to do with a lizard in the tub?"

"She saw some wildlife program on TV about these lizards. They apparently eat seven times their body weight in bugs every day. She figured that buying four of them would save a lot of time, money and trouble in the long run."

"So she bought four lizards and turned them loose in the house?"

"Yes. I know it sounds peculiar, but it really wasn't such a bad idea."

"Oh, come on."

"The problem was that we seemed to have gotten a deviant batch. They're usually supposed to be quite harmless and peaceful, but ours were positively vicious. Luckily they didn't last too long. Two ran away, one died of a mysterious illness—"

"Leah, this is a ridiculous story."

"Consider the source." Their eyes met and they started laughing. It was a long while before Leah could say, "Anyhow, I thought they were all long since dead and gone. This one must have been eating well. He's a lot bigger than I remember."

"I wonder how he got into the bathtub."

"I wonder how we're going to get him out."

"And what are we going to do with him once he's out?" Adam added. "I'm not jumpy, but I don't relish the thought of finding him in my bed or under my desk in a day or two. He's not like the Questing Beast. He's distinctly antisocial."

Neither of them wanted to kill a living thing, even such an unpleasant one. They agreed that killing it would, in any case, somehow be a violation of Verbena's trust.

Leah said that little boys often enjoyed grotesque pets. Adam pointed out that they didn't know any little boys in the area, and anyhow, no mother would appreciate their giving a cranky lizard to her son.

At last they agreed that the best course of action would be to set it free down by the stream and let it fend for itself. Leah worried guiltily that it might die during the winter, but Adam thought it might hibernate like a snake.

Once they had gathered two pairs of gardening gloves, a big fishing net, a cat carrier and a spray can of ether, they went back into the bathroom.

"Just stun it, don't poison it," Leah cautioned when Adam sprayed ether into the lizard's hissing face.

"Relax." He watched it for a minute. "Quick. Hand me the net."

The dizzy lizard struggled a bit, but they managed to get him from the tub into the net and then from the net into the cat carrier. They congratulated each other, and then carried him out to the stream at the back of the property.

He woke up on the way. If the scuffling noises inside the carrier were any indication, he was pretty annoyed with both of them.

"Be careful," Leah warned as Adam unlatched the door of the cat carrier. "He might jump out at you."

When their captive scrambled through the grass and disappeared down the banks of the stream, Leah cheered and gripped Adam's arm with both hands. "What teamwork!"

He grinned and looked down at her, then caught his breath. Her cheeks were flushed, her dark eyes were sparkling and her whole face was alight with laughter. She had never looked lovelier. Following his impulses, he pulled her closer and lowered his mouth to hers.

She was rigid with surprise for a moment, then she answered his warm kiss, opening her mouth to his questing tongue and snuggling closer into his embrace.

He kissed her till her mind spun, then pulled away to nuzzle her hair and rub his cheek against hers in a gesture so affectionate it made her heart swell.

When he looked down into her face, he smiled and brushed her hair away from her forehead. "You look all messy."

"I've wrestled an alligator this morning."

"*I* wrestled. You coached."

"I was with you in spirit."

He kissed her lightly again.

She felt good about him and about this. But she wondered if she would later. With that thought in mind, she stepped out of his embrace and said, "I've got a load of errands to run today."

"Need help?" He turned to accompany her as she started walking back toward the house. He knew she had already made what she considered an enormous concession; he wouldn't push her.

"No, I can manage."

Ten minutes later she asked him if he needed anything from the stores in town, said goodbye and drove off. She knew that somehow a silly adventure with a lizard and a few kisses by the stream had wrought an enormous change between them, and she didn't know what to do about it.

She was unpacking groceries in the kitchen that afternoon when the phone rang.

"Hello?" she said, balancing the receiver between her shoulder and ear as she pushed a cat away from the fresh produce.

"To whom am I speaking?" asked a male voice.

On the outside chance that it might be an obscene phone call, Leah demanded, "Who is this?"

"I'm a friend of Mordred McCargar."

"Oh. I'm afraid he's not here."

"Can you tell me when you expect him?"

A prickly feeling ran down Leah's spine. "We don't expect him at all." She wondered where Mordred was at this moment.

"Are you quite sure?"

"What is this about?" she said. She started to suspect this man wasn't a friend of Mordred's at all.

There was a long silence. "If he should turn up, ma'am, I would appreciate you notifying me."

"If you're a friend of his, why should *I* be the one to notify you?"

"I'm sorry to have to tell you that he's in a bit of trouble. I'm afraid he may be reluctant to accept my help."

"Why?"

"Let me give you a number where I can be reached."

"No!" Leah said, suddenly feeling a little frightened.

"Ma'am—"

"And don't call here again!" She slammed the receiver down with such force it fell off the hook.

As she stooped to pick it up, she heard Adam's voice behind her. "Something wrong?"

"No!" She realized her voice sounded shrill. She cleared her throat and repeated, "No."

"I heard you halfway down the hall. Usually *I'm* the only person you talk to that way." His eyes were watchful and alert. She turned away. "Who was it, Leah?"

"I don't know," she answered truthfully.

"What did he want?"

She shrugged. "Wrong number."

"Leah." His tone indicated he knew she was lying.

"You'd better go feed the raccoons," she said. "Remember how I told you they overreact when they don't get fed?"

For a moment she thought he would press the issue. Then, reluctantly, he pushed his way out the back door and trotted down the porch steps. She let out her breath and sank into a chair.

The phone rang again.

She stared at it for seven rings before she finally picked up the receiver. She held it away from her ear as if it could bite her.

"Hello?" she said faintly.

"Leah, is that you? This is Melchior Browning."

"Oh, Melchior," she said in relief, "what can I do for you?"

"I heard Verbena left town due to a sudden emergency. Anything serious?"

"An old friend of hers will be operated on sometime soon and she wanted to be there," Leah explained.

"I see. I hope all goes well."

"Thank you."

"Verbena mentioned a couple of books she wanted to loan me before I left town. I was hoping I could stop by this week to pick them up."

"Yes, of course," Leah said. They arranged a time later in the week.

It was only after she hung up that Leah realized that Mordred, apparently on the run from someone, didn't even know that his father was ill in London and that Verbena needed his moral support.

Leah didn't want whoever was after Mordred to catch him. She didn't want to be deprived of the chance to give him a good thrashing herself.

Seven

Leah's refusal to confide in Adam about the phone call put a slight rift between them, but they were still joined by a new bond born of the responsibilities they were sharing in Verbena's chaotic household. They had also stopped trying to pretend the sexual chemistry between them didn't exist.

Leah was skittish because she didn't know what to do about it. And Adam treated her with a subtle tenderness for the next few days that made her feel as if she would crack like fine crystal before much more time passed.

They hadn't argued for days. What's more, she could clearly see that, like her, he wasn't sleeping well at night. She wished that Verbena would come home. For the first time since her childhood, she wanted Verbena to protect *her*. From what? She wasn't sure. But Adam was destroying her equilibrium as no one and nothing had ever done before.

"Leah? Are you ever going to come out of here?"

"Yahh!" She nearly jumped out of her skin when Adam stuck his head into the study and spoke to her.

He looked around, as if trying to figure out what had frightened her.

"Sorry," she said faintly. "I was...concentrating."

"Uh-huh." He came into the room. "Leah, I admire diligence, but you've been in here since before I woke up. You didn't come out for lunch or dinner. It's nearly midnight. Don't you think you should take a break?"

Leah shrugged and put down her notebook. "Yes, maybe you're right." She stretched and then grimaced as her body protested.

"Stiff? I'm not surprised." He moved to stand behind her and started rubbing her shoulders.

"Ohh," she moaned. She dropped her head forward as his massaging fingers eased away the tensions of too much study, too much emotional pressure and too little sleep. "You have magic hands."

"I've been told that before," he said complacently.

She stiffened.

"Relax," he chided. "Your shoulders are as hard as rock, Leah." He leaned over her shoulder and said, "Want me to walk on your back?"

"I think not, Adam," she said dryly.

"How's your work going?" he asked, continuing to knead her shoulders.

After a slight hesitation, she admitted reluctantly, "Not too well."

"What's wrong?"

She frowned discontentedly. "Well, I got ahold of the sources Melchior Browning recommended."

"And?"

She shrugged. "They're just not what I wanted. One was written at least two centuries after the period I'm researching, so it's accuracy is highly questionable. The other is just too general to be of any use."

"Ah, so Melchior isn't perfect, after all?"

She shifted uncomfortably, not wanting to bring up that argument again.

"Since you're too stubborn to ask for help, I'll offer it out of the goodness of my heart," Adam said as his hands slowly worked their way down her spine.

"You mentioned a series of letters in Middle English in the British Museum," she said humbly.

"Yes. I have a good contact there. I'll call tomorrow and ask her to make copies and send them home with Verbena for you."

"That's ... very nice of you, Adam."

"In the meantime, I can think of at least one book that ought to be in the university library that might help you. I'll write the title down for you."

"I really appreciate this, Adam. Especially after I..." She let the sentence trail off awkwardly, not quite sure how to finish it. Instead she said, "Unfortunately, it happens to be a subject Verbena doesn't know much about."

"Then it's one of the few. That woman has memorized more research than most people have ever even read," Adam said admiringly.

"She is an extraordinary fountain of knowledge," Leah agreed.

"And remarkably skilled at interpreting the evidence."

"Yes." She closed her eyes dreamily as his warm, strong hands soothed and comforted her.

She was practically dozing when he finally stopped. He leaned forward, wrapped his arms around her and whispered, "I think it's time for you to go to bed."

"Yes," she murmured sleepily.

He kissed her ear. "Want me to carry you?"

That woke her up. "No." She stood. "Thanks, I'll manage. Good night, Adam. Thanks for the massage. And the help."

She didn't stop talking until she was out the door, and Adam had the feeling that she would practically run to her bedroom.

He didn't think she was afraid of him, but she was afraid of something. Or at least she was reluctant to take the next step in their relationship. It could be any one of a dozen reasons. She still didn't approve of him, despite their growing closeness. She was also definitely keeping some kind of secret from him—and from Verbena, he suspected.

He prowled restlessly around the study, trying to find some way to chase away his frustration. He almost wished the ferret would escape again. A good swift chase through the countryside would be just the thing.

But he wanted to chase Leah. And when he caught her, they would...

Arrgh, why her? he wondered irritably. He shoved Macbeth out of his way and stalked out of the room. He'd go out for a midnight run anyhow, ferret or no ferret.

"Another restless night," he muttered.

Jenny Harper showed up with her exorcist the next afternoon.

"I thought she'd bring a priest," Adam whispered to Leah.

"No. Jenny's terribly New Age," Leah whispered back.

"Leah. Adam. *This* is Ralu," said Jenny importantly.

"Hi. Nice dress," said Adam.

Leah stepped on his foot. Ralu was garbed in about thirty yards of white linen. It surrounded her several times, spread in a wide pool at her feet and then dragged behind her for a few yards. It was going to get filthy by the time Ralu finished walking through Verbena's house, Leah reflected.

"Pleased to meet you," Leah said.

Ralu drew a deep breath and closed her eyes. After a ponderous moment, she said, "Yes. You are."

Leah and Adam exchanged a glance.

"But *it* is not," Ralu declared.

With one arm extended before her, she swept through the house without another word. The rest of them trailed after her. By the time they reached the staircase, Ralu was halfway to the second floor.

"Isn't she remarkable?" whispered Jenny in awe.

"Incredible," said Adam.

"Unbelievable," said Leah.

"In fact, I think I can honestly say I've never seen anyone like her in my life," said Adam.

"Come on," said Jenny excitedly, dashing up the stairs.

Leah glanced at Adam. His eyes sparkled. "I wouldn't miss this for the world," he said. "Are you coming?"

She shook her head. "Melchior Browning is coming over to borrow a few of Verbena's books."

He shrugged. "Then it's just as well I have something to entertain me while he's here." He trotted up the steps after their guests.

Melchior arrived about ten minutes later. It took Leah only a few minutes to find the books he wanted. Verbena's bookshelves, at least, were well organized.

"And how is your research coming, my dear? Were the sources I mentioned what you were looking for?"

"Yes," Leah lied. "Thank you for your time and help."

"It is an interesting topic. As is the subject of your aunt's book. It's about the medieval custom of consigning women to the convent, whether they were suited to that life or not, isn't it?"

Leah's heart sank when Melchior sat down and made himself comfortable, evidently prepared for a nice, long chat. She wanted to get him out of the house before Adam came back downstairs.

"That's part of the subject," Leah conceded. "Verbena says the bulk of the book will study how those women adapted to the veil, or how they made that life adapt to their needs, and how this in turn affected perceptions about nuns in various communities in the Middle Ages."

"Yes..." Melchior gave her a significant look. "It's a pity your aunt has chosen such a, shall we say, *undistinguished* partner for such an exciting project."

Leah felt her spine stiffen involuntarily. She couldn't fathom the sudden offense she had taken at his comment.

Particularly since she was usually so adamant about Adam's unsuitability.

They heard a sudden piercing wail from the top floor of the house.

"Good heavens!" said Melchior.

A moment later they heard two female voices chanting something indistinguishable.

"What on earth is going on here?" Melchior demanded.

"It's...a long story." He waited expectantly. She kept stubbornly silent. She assumed that Adam would remain upstairs as long as the chanting continued, but how long would that be? If only she hadn't firmly locked the back door, the dogs could stampede into the room and convince Melchior to depart posthaste.

Once he realized that she wasn't going to offer an explanation about the weird noises emanating from the third floor of the house, Melchior resumed talking about history.

Since Leah was dividing her attention between him and the sounds of exorcism, she was only half-conscious of what he was saying.

"The University of Padua. A noble and ancient institution with which I have intimate ties."

"Uh-huh," she responded inelegantly.

Now that she gave it some thought, it did seem strange that Melchior Browning of Iowa should speak with a pseudo-British accent. She froze as the chanting stopped. Would the exorcism continue, or would they all be coming downstairs momentarily?

"But, of course, I lacked sufficient time to pursue that line of inquiry. I regret that a man in my position has so many demands on his time."

And that natty tweed jacket with suede elbow patches. Why on earth would anyone walk around in that jacket on a hot summer day in the country?

"Of course, I would be only too happy to lend Verbena the benefit of my experience..."

"What?" she said suddenly.

"On the book."

"*Licentious Nuns*?" He gave her a puzzled look. "I mean, *A Viable Alternative*?" she amended.

"Yes, that's what I've been saying," he said a trifle impatiently.

Was that the sound of footsteps on the stairs? No, no, perhaps not. "When did she ask for your assistance?" Leah asked politely.

"Well, she hasn't yet."

"Then why—?"

"Obviously she will be looking for a new collaborator."

"Obviously?"

"You have told her about Mr. Jordan, haven't you?"

"I . . . No."

He suddenly looked very annoyed. "In heaven's name, why not?"

She frowned at him, not liking his tone of voice. "I beg your pardon?"

"I said, why haven't you exposed the scoundrel to your aunt?"

She stared at him in amazement as realization slowly dawned. "I assumed, Professor, that you gave me that information in confidence."

That flustered him for a moment. "Of course I did. But surely your aunt is included in your confidence."

"Why didn't you tell her yourself, if it's that important?"

He avoided answering the question by saying impatiently, "Of course it's that important! You must tell her at once!"

Leah narrowed her eyes. "And when I tell her, she'll dump him. You'll come over to comfort her and just naturally wind up filling his place. Is that the idea, Professor?"

"I don't care for your tone, young lady," he said imperiously.

"But telling her about him yourself would be too obvious, wouldn't it? So you used me. You *used* me."

"You're making a big mis—"

"Am I? In order to speak to me privately, you lured me to the university under the pretence of advising me on a topic you know absolutely nothing about." She slapped her forehead. "No wonder those sources were so useless!"

"How dare you accuse me of such a thing!"

"And on top of that, here you sit insisting I bother Verbena with this now, when she's in the middle of a personal crisis. What kind of a person are you?"

"I used to wonder that," said Adam from the doorway.

Leah whirled to see him and Jenny supporting Ralu, who had evidently been through a transforming experience. "Is she all right?" Leah asked.

"Nothing that a few years of rehabilitation won't cure," Adam said. "Come on, let's help her to a chair, Jenny."

"I refuse to stay here and be insulted!" said Melchior.

"By all means, don't let me keep you," Leah said coldly. "And please leave those books here. I don't think Verbena would want to loan them to you, after all."

"What?" he exclaimed.

"Don't take it so hard, Melchior. They're pretty dull anyhow," Adam said amiably as he deposited Ralu into an easy chair.

"*You're* responsible for this!" Melchior looked apoplectic as he pointed an accusing finger at Adam.

"Leave him alone!" Leah said angrily. Both men turned to stare at her. Adam looked more surprised than Melchior.

After a moment of stunned silence all the way around the room, Adam said, "Well, this *has* been an exciting day."

"You will be sorry about this, young woman!" Melchior threatened.

"I doubt it, Melchior," Adam said placidly. "I'm living proof that you personally can't keep a good man down."

"And you," cried Melchior, turning on Adam, "have no business calling yourself a doctor."

"I don't call myself a doctor. But I find it ironic that you of all people should say that to me."

Their eyes locked and held. Melchior backed down first. He left without another word. The roar of his car as he drove off was like a parting insult. Adam shrugged and turned his attention to Leah.

"To think I should live to see you act as my champion. You were magnificent."

She avoided his warm, probing gaze. When had her loyalties shifted so dramatically? she wondered. Nothing about Adam had changed. But the way she felt about him certainly had, she acknowledged uncomfortably.

"Extraordinary!" cried Ralu suddenly, drawing everyone's attention. "A force, a power, an energy—"

"What is this, a car commercial?" said Adam.

"Shhh," said Jenny. "She's coming out of her trance."

"Oh. Want a shot of whiskey, Ralu?" he asked instead.

"Adam, really," Leah chided.

"Ralu doesn't pollute her body with alcohol," Jenny said reverently.

"Could've fooled me," Adam muttered.

After considerable theatrics, Ralu finally stood upright, opened her eyes and spoke to them in a normal voice.

"So is our... intruder gone?" Leah asked hopefully.

Ralu inhaled deeply. "No. It is a force of compelling strength."

"You can't get rid of it?" Leah asked worriedly. Who would keep Verbena's house clean if Jenny didn't come back to work?

Ralu glared at Leah in indignation. "Of course I can get rid... *escort* it across the void. But it will take several encounters. Today was just the beginning."

"You'll be back? What do you do for an encore?" Adam said.

Ralu smiled seductively at him and clasped his hands between hers. "Your unwavering support, in those moments when I grappled with darkness, was invaluable, Adam." Then she glanced dismissively at Leah. "You should try to erase your prejudices, my dear."

"She likes me better than you," Adam said smugly to Leah as Ralu prepared to leave the house.

"That's a dubious distinction," Leah answered dryly. She followed Ralu and Jenny into the entrance hall. "Uh, Ralu. Just how many more encounters will we need?"

"That is not for *me* to say," said Ralu portentously.

"Who does say?" Leah persisted.

"My secretary will send you my bill when the process has been completed." Ralu sailed out the door with Jenny in hot pursuit.

"What do you suppose she charges?" Leah murmured morosely.

"Your first-born child?" Adam suggested.

"Go away. Leave me in peace."

"You missed all the action up there. Of course, there seems to have been quite a lot of action down here, too."

Their eyes met. His were warm, curious, hopeful. She felt shattered by what had just happened with Melchior. Of course, the man was obviously a jerk, reputation or no reputation. She probably would have thrown him out anyhow when she realized how he had used her and how little he really cared about Verbena's needs.

But she had been most deeply offended by his open contempt for Adam. And now Adam stood looking at her with those big blue bedroom eyes, waiting for her to explain why she had defended him so vehemently against a man she had professed to admire.

"Leah, don't you think you and I—"

"I'm going to the library," she said suddenly.

"What?"

"I called the university, and they said they have that book you recommended to me. Silly me. I forgot all about it in all the excitement.'' She was already scooping up her purse and the car keys as she spoke. ''Don't hold dinner, I'll probably stay there late to do some reading in their reference section.''

''Leah, we need to talk.''

The phone rang suddenly. He looked from her to the ringing phone in the next room and back again with an almost comical look of frustration. She froze for a moment. Mordred's ''friend''? Mordred himself? She trailed nervously after Adam as he strode into the next room to pick up the phone. After a moment, he covered the receiver with his hand and looked at her.

''It's my publisher.'' His eyes asked her not to leave.

''Bye, Adam,'' she said with unconvincing casualness and escaped out the front door.

At the library, she checked out the book she wanted. Then she spent about five useless hours in the reference section. There was plenty of material, but it all swam before her eyes, becoming hopelessly entangled with ever-changing images of the irreverent, grinning, golden pagan god who haunted her nights and enlivened her days. She took a short dinner break, then sat pushing her food around her plate while her mind continued to dally with the object of her obsession.

She had been infatuated before, and once, while working on her master's degree, she had even thought she might be in love. But she had never felt like this about a man. And she had *never* let a man disrupt her studies before.

Adam Jordan, of all people! He was the antithesis of everything she worked for, respected and believed in. He even sailed under false colors, she thought morosely. Despite her new antipathy toward Melchior, she still had to believe his story. Adam himself had admitted that he had never finished his Ph.D. program. Yet her aunt, and a number of other people, believed he possessed a degree from Barrington University, and he let them go on believing it.

As she drove home, she remembered suddenly that she had refused to listen to his side of the story. She wondered, without real hope, if he could possibly exonerate himself. The closer she got to the house, the more important that question became. By the time she pulled into the driveway, she was determined to seek him out and ask him without further delay.

The ferret was waiting for her as she entered the front door, but she was getting to be as fast as he was. She blocked him with her foot, scooped him up in one arm and slammed the front door.

"Leah? Is that you?" Adam called from the second floor.

"Yes!"

"Can you come up here for a minute? I need your advice."

That surprised her enough to make her lose sight of her own goals for a moment. She trotted up the stairs and walked down the hall to his bedroom with King John cradled in her arms. What she saw was so surprising that she stopped dead in her tracks and nearly squeezed the life out of the protesting ferret.

Adam's room was spotlessly clean. That alone was surprising enough. In addition, his closet and all his dresser drawers were open. He was pulling clothes out at random and haphazardly stuffing them into a small suitcase.

"You're leaving?" she blurted out. A sense of loss overwhelmed her.

"Do you think I should wear a tie?" he asked, frowning at a threadbare brown necktie as he turned it over in his hands.

She failed to see the connection between sartorial elegance and his desertion. "You're leaving?" she repeated.

"I hate ties. I never wear ties. But I *will* be asking for a lot of money, and maybe I should look, you know, more formidable. What do you think?"

She ripped the frayed necktie out of his hands. That got his full attention. King John squirmed nervously. "Where are you going?"

"Manhattan."

She looked at the suitcase, noticing that it was really just an overnight bag. She should have realized that it was too small for him to be moving out. "You're going to see your publisher?" she asked suddenly.

"Yes. So what do you think about the tie?"

"When are you leaving?"

"Tomorrow morning."

"So soon?" she asked in dismay. She wouldn't have spent all evening by herself if she had known he would be leaving in the morning, she thought desperately.

"Yes. That was what they were calling about."

"How long will you be gone?"

"Three days. So do you think—"

"Three days? Why didn't you tell me?" she demanded.

"Because you ran out the door and spent the rest of the day avoiding me," he flared.

"Force of habit." She set the ferret down on the floor and regarded the necktie in her hands. "Adam, you can't wear this. It's so old and frayed, they'll think you're either desperate for money or deliberately insulting them."

"Oh." He shrugged dismissively. "Then I guess I won't wear a tie."

"You could *buy* a tie," she suggested in exasperation.

"I'll think about it." He turned away and resumed packing.

Leah stood in the center of the room watching him. She folded her hands. She unfolded her hands. She started to leave, then decided to stay. When he turned abruptly to speak to her, she nearly jumped out of her skin.

"What's the matter with you?" he demanded.

"Nothing."

He came to stand before her. His expression softened a little. "I'm sorry about leaving you stuck with the menagerie and Ralu."

"That's okay," she mumbled.

"Are you afraid to be here alone?" he asked suddenly.

"No, of course not." She looked at the floor.

"Leah." His voice was soft. He tilted her chin up, forcing her to meet his probing gaze. "What's wrong, then?"

To her mortification, her voice trembled as she repeated, "Nothing."

His eyes relentlessly searched hers, demanding the truth. "What's wrong?" he repeated with soft insistence.

As if moved more by his will than her own, she whispered, "You're going away."

She had thought for a moment he might look puzzled or, worse, smug. But his eyes grew tender and his smile was gentle. "Will you miss me?" he murmured.

"Yes," she admitted reluctantly.

"You don't sound too sure," he growled.

"I'm . . . surprised."

"So am I, frankly. When did it happen?" His hand touched hers, slid up her arm and drew her closer.

"I don't know exactly." Her voice was tight.

"I don't know exactly, either." His other hand came up to touch her face. "But I can't help it." He tilted her chin up for his kiss.

"Neither can I," she admitted an instant before his mouth closed over hers.

Their lips met with a sweet magic that turned suddenly to sultry passion as their arms slid around each other and their mouths moved hungrily together. His hands stroked down her back, up her shoulders, into her hair, then moved restlessly down her back again, pulling her closer.

She parted her lips on a sigh, and his warm, silky tongue slipped between them. He tickled the roof of her mouth as his firm lips rubbed moistly across hers. She curled her tongue up to touch his, stroking and caressing it, then chasing it back into the honeyed sweetness of his mouth. Nothing had ever tasted as good as he did, and she explored his mouth boldly, enjoying the sounds of arousal he made deep in his throat.

He tightened a steel-banded arm around her waist to lift her slightly. Leah arched her back, pressing her breasts against his chest and closing her eyes as pleasure swept through her.

He kissed her neck, her cheek, her shoulder, trailing his lips across her smooth skin with moist fire. Her arms clutched at his shoulders, and wonder pierced through her at the supple iron-hard strength she felt there. She rubbed her cheek against his softly waving hair as he rained questing kisses across her exposed flesh, tasting and exploring.

He murmured her name, and she sought his mouth with her own, starving for the taste and feel of his kiss, greedily searching out the pleasure his passion gave her.

They kissed as if they couldn't get enough of each other, as if every second of longing could be satisfied in that one moment when their mouths melded together and their tongues mated with delirious delight.

Then suddenly he slid his hands off her body and up her arms. He ended their kiss and pulled her caressing hands down and clasped them tightly in his. He brought their joined hands to rest between their bodies, separating them.

Stunned by the force and speed with which he had ended their embrace, Leah's eyes flew open and met his gaze questioningly. His own eyes were dark with passion, but filled with concern and a few questions of his own.

"Why—?" She felt too breathless, too moved, to continue the question, but she held his gaze. She might be crazy, but she wanted this and she wouldn't—*couldn't*—pretend otherwise.

He released one of her hands to reach up and touch her cheek. He traced his forefinger lightly across her lower lip. She shuddered with longing.

"I think 'why' is my question," he whispered unsteadily. "Why tonight? I've wanted to . . . touch you ever since you came here, and you've looked at me like I was the devil's own spawn."

"I'm sorry," she said. She meant it.

He spread his hand across her neck and rubbed it gently. His eyes told her he didn't really want to talk right now, but he persisted in a husky voice, "Why did you defend me today?"

Confusion and desire assailed her with equal force, and the result was that she suddenly felt ridiculously close to tears.

He tangled his hand in her hair and drew her head back. "Why?"

She made a helpless sound and shook her head. "I don't know," she whispered.

And because he could see it was the truth, because he knew they had both pondered enough and needed only to feel for a while, he gave it up for the moment. Instead he kissed her softly on the lips and said, "I want to make love to you."

She stared at him with wide, serious dark eyes and said nothing.

"Do you think, as a favor to me," he said in a strained voice, "you could possibly make up your mind in the next few seconds?"

That made her smile, and he suddenly knew that, whatever her motivations, everything would be all right. She lowered her eyes in a shy gesture he found both seductive and endearing.

"Leah?" He started to pull her closer.

"The light," she murmured.

The moon was shining. Its brightness would spill across his bed when they turned out the light, so he was willing to give in to her request. He pulled her across the room to the light switch. He turned off the big overhead light and closed the bedroom door.

"Just so the Questing Beast won't join us later," he said.

They stood staring at each other for a moment, full of sweet anticipation, aware that tonight was going to be the culmination of a lot of seemingly futile fantasies.

Adam glanced toward the bed. "I've thought night after night about seeing you in that bed." He slid his hands over her shoulders and tunneled them into her long hair. "With your hair spread over the pillows. Or over my chest." Leah drew in a sharp breath. He slid his hands down her back and pressed her against the hard length of his body. "I've thought about you lying there in the moonlight, warm and soft, by my side, in my arms . . . beneath me."

She made a small inarticulate sound and slid her arms around him. She pressed her mouth against his neck and then, knowing what he most needed to hear, she whispered, "So have I."

He planted kisses along her shoulder and neck. "You don't mind?"

She slid her palms up and down his chest. "Being the object of your fantasies?"

"Hmm." He guided her hand to the buttons of his shirt.

"No, no..." And then he pulled her cotton blouse out of the waistband of her skirt and slid his hands underneath to caress her. Unaware of the change in her words, she started murmuring, "Yes, yes . . ."

His palms were warm, so warm, sending heat shafting through her body and making every nerve ending come brilliantly alive. His hot kisses, his clever hands, the subtle rhythm of his body against hers, bewitched her. When he started to undress her, her hands shook so much with excitement that she couldn't finish unbuttoning his shirt. He chuckled with pleasure, drew her hands back to him and urged her to keep trying.

After a few buttons and far too many kisses to count, Leah finally pushed his shirt off his shoulders and let it fall to the floor. He was much swifter than she, and her blouse and skirt joined his shirt in a crumpled heap within moments. He admired her flimsy undergarments for a moment and then, with animal grace, he scooped her up in his arms and carried her over to the bed.

As soon as her head touched the pillows, Adam's body covered hers with hungry possessiveness. He kissed her long and hard before finally pulling back to look at her.

He spread her hair over her pillow. He looked big and godlike as he rested above her, propped up on his arms. The moonlight cast a silvery sheen over his golden skin and hair, and he was indeed a fairy-tale lover in that moment.

He brushed her fanned-out hair with his hands. "You look just like I pictured you." He sat up and let his eyes trail smokily down her body. "Except for this," he murmured. He lifted her easily with one arm and unclasped her bra faster and more efficiently than she could have done it herself. She decided this was no time to dwell on nasty suspicions, so she let his expertise with women's undergarments pass without comment. "And this." He peeled off her panties with ease and tossed them over his shoulder.

"Oh, Leah." He sighed as he looked down at her. He laced the fingers of one hand with hers. After another moment, he lifted her hand to his lips and kissed it. "My imagination didn't begin to do you justice."

He pulled her up to a sitting position. He slid his hands down her breasts and softly teased the pink tips with his thumbs in an exploratory caress. Her nipples peaked under his gentle hands, growing hard and rosy almost instantly. She sighed luxuriantly and touched his cheek.

Suddenly he pressed his open mouth against hers, his kiss so forceful it pushed her back down into the pillows. He pulled away and scowled at her. "I've been going crazy imagining this! Why didn't you come in here *days* ago?"

She had to laugh at the moral outrage in his voice. He grinned sheepishly and let her roll him over in the pillows. They kissed again and nuzzled each other, enjoying each other immensely. She slid her legs against his and frowned at the rough denim she felt there. Her hand yanked demandingly at his belt.

"Yow! Be careful," he warned between gritted teeth. "Everything's all sort of jammed up in there right now."

She laughed again. She had never expected to feel this passionate and this full of fun at the same time, but she didn't question it. Everything was special when she did it with Adam. She started trying to unfasten his jeans. His kisses made her clumsy.

She jerked futilely at the zipper. Adam gasped. His voice was very, very tight when he said, "Maybe I should do that, Leah."

She sat up. "No. I want to. Just hold still for a minute."

He squirmed. Then he gasped again. "I *can't* hold still with you fiddling like that."

She grinned. "What? Like this?"

He grabbed her teasing hands and pulled her back down to the pillows for a violent kiss. Then he rolled off the bed and unfastened his jeans himself. He met her eyes for a moment, then pushed his pants off his hips, kicked them aside and stood naked before her.

Leah swallowed. He was stunning, like any wild creature, like any untamed male. He was strong and beautiful and hard everywhere, golden and gleaming and perfect. Her eyes dropped to the denser hair below his navel, to the earthy longing that she had stirred in him. She satisfied her curiosity by observing that not all of his hair was golden. He let her stare, natural and unashamed.

And then the moment for looking had passed, and they both wanted to touch, wanted it so badly their hands couldn't seem to rest in any one place. They rolled across the bed together, tangling the sheets and knocking pillows to the floor. He touched her boldly, without caution or coyness, seeking out every secret he wanted to learn, and encouraging her to do the same with him.

He lowered his mouth to her breasts and tasted her roseate nipples with his velvety tongue, laving first one, then the other while Leah ran her hands over his back and kissed his hair. He drew one hard, wet peak into his hot mouth and sucked firmly. Her back arched off the bed and she moaned low and loudly. She writhed against him, twisted the sheets with her hands, scratched his back with her nails, and he responded to her desperation by tugging even more deeply on her breast.

She was sobbing when he stopped, feeling shredded by her desires. She kissed him with ruthless urgency and pushed her hips against his, feeling further inflamed by the hot shaft that rubbed against her thighs.

"Please." Her voice was so choked she didn't know if he could understand her. She didn't understand the feverish words he muttered against her lips as he kissed her again and again.

He slid his hands over her smooth stomach and down to the silky triangle of hair between her thighs. She gasped and heard herself pleading shamelessly with him to make love to her. His fingers probed delicately to investigate the mystery of the wet heat between her thighs.

She could tell that what he found there inflamed him as much as his touch inflamed her. "For me, Leah... hot like this for me," he whispered, drowning her with hungry kisses.

"Yes, yes, yes..."

And then he slid her hips between hers. She felt him enter her with a strong, deep thrust. Her hands slid automatically down to his bottom. She dug her fingers into his tensed muscles and pulled him farther inside her as she raised her hips to meet his next thrust.

He pushed and she arched, again and again. They made a very tight fit. Just perfect, she thought blissfully.

And then she felt him as deep as he could go, so much a part of her that her breath, her heartbeat, her very life, seemed inextricably entwined with his. He pulled away, and in sudden reflex, she wrapped her legs around him.

Adam made love as he did everything else, with total absorption, with abandon, with commitment and with impressive strength.

She sensed that he sought to hold back, to make it last, but she had lost all track of time, all awareness of another world around them. All she knew or thought or felt was his hot, damp body gliding in beautiful motion against hers, the bunch and flow of his muscles under her hands, the hoarse words he rasped against her skin, the hot kisses he spread across her face and the hard, urgent heat he spread through her.

They rose and fell together in ecstasy, soaring a little higher and sinking a little deeper each time. Finally their senses were so tautly strung on the rack of pleasure they themselves had created that they couldn't stand their magnificent mutual torture a moment longer. Leah trembled and cried out as her whole body flooded with a release of rich pleasure.

And even as her body shredded her soul with delight, she felt the only other thing in the world that could have given her as much pleasure. With one more fierce thrust, Adam shuddered and sank down against her, moaning her name again and again as the pleasure he had sought to give Leah overwhelmed him and claimed him as its willing prisoner, too.

Eight

———

It seemed that before Leah had even had time to contemplate the folly of what she had done, Adam's hands were sliding up her thighs and his lips were on hers. And she wanted him again, needing him as fiercely as if the previous hour had happened an eon ago.

And so they made love, in silence this time, their harsh breathing and tortured sighs the only sounds they made to compete with the rustle of leaves in the wind and the song of the crickets they could hear through the open windows.

When it was over and Leah's spinning universe subsided, she found that they had wound up lying with their heads at the foot of the bed. Adam stretched out an arm toward a discarded pillow, and they shared it, too exhausted to even scoot back up to the head of the bed.

He folded his arms around her and she nestled against him, her contentment so great that no thought could disturb it. She didn't think she had ever felt this relaxed in her whole life.

Adam rolled on his side to study her face. This, too, was Leah, he thought in wonder.

Intelligent, critical, loyal, demanding, funny, exasperating, brave, committed—these qualities he had already come to know and accept in her. He had long suspected her vulnerability and tenderness. He had guessed she was passionate and sensual underneath her intellectual, self-reliant manner. He was amazed and delighted to discover a wildness in her that he had never imagined, had never experienced before.

And this, too, was Leah, snuggled up next to him in warm, drowsy contentment, affectionate, gentle, womanly, giving. His eyes traveled over her tangled hair, flushed face and slightly swollen lips. She stirred up his heart. His body, he acknowledged wryly, had taken about as much stirring up as it could stand for the moment, and he suspected that hers had, too.

"Why are you smiling?" she murmured drowsily.

"I feel good." He kissed her forehead. "No, I feel great."

"So do I."

"You look all messy. But you still look perfect. How do you do that?" he teased.

"It's the sign of a superior character."

He grunted.

"Why is your room so clean?" she asked.

"I couldn't possibly get any work done after you left today," he said significantly.

"Neither could I," she admitted. "I read two hundred pages at the library without absorbing a single word."

"That's what you get for denying your baser instincts," he chided. "It never works out."

"No, I think that's what I get for denying *your* baser instincts."

"Well, I forgive you," he said magnanimously.

"Thanks a lot." She was silent for a few minutes before she said softly, "Adam?"

"Hmm?" He trailed his hands over her body with affection and curiosity rather than passion.

After a slight pause, she said, "I'm glad. That I came in here tonight, I mean."

"So am I." He kissed her and hugged her tightly. "So am I."

"I just…don't want you to think I'm going to try to, you know, squirm out of it and say it was all your idea."

"I know you wouldn't do that. If there's one thing I can usually count on from you, it's frankness."

"Yes."

Her voice was soft and uneasy. He could tell that she was reluctant to bring up myriad personal subjects between them. He had a dozen questions he wanted to ask, and a dozen things he wanted to tell her. But not wanting to shatter the harmony of the moment, he decided to go after a harmless subject instead.

"What's this?" he whispered, tracing a small, faint scar on her stomach.

She smiled. "Appendix."

"How old were you?"

"Nine. Incredible as it sounds, my father rushed me to the emergency room, and when he gave them our name, they said my mother had brought in my little sister just an hour earlier for the same problem. Talk about catastrophe."

"You have a sister?" Adam asked in surprise. Neither she nor Verbena had ever mentioned a sister.

Leah's smile faded. "She died with my parents."

Adam's wandering hands stilled on her body. He knew the accident that had taken her parents' lives had happened some fifteen years ago, but he didn't know if Leah would nevertheless resent his asking about it.

She lowered her head and rested it against his chest. He stroked her back, silently encouraging her to tell him.

"It was a car accident, you know. I was twelve, almost thirteen."

He could tell by the tone of her voice and the rigid set of her spine that there was more to the story than that.

"Where were they going?"

"Dinner. They were taking my little sister out for dinner. It was her tenth birthday."

He frowned, puzzled. He tried to keep his voice neutral. "Why didn't you go with them?"

There was no answer.

"Were you with friends?"

"No." Her voice was low.

He sensed that she wanted to tell him the rest but needed his help.

"Were you sick?"

She shook her head.

"I...don't understand." He held her tightly so she would know that, whatever she said, it wouldn't change his feelings about her.

She sat up suddenly. She was dry-eyed, but her face was drawn and tense. She met his eyes as she finished her story.

"It was Saturday. I went to a carnival with a bunch of my friends. My little sister, Sarah, had gone with us. I was supposed to watch out for her, but I didn't. I didn't want to take care of her, I just wanted to have fun with my friends. So I brushed her off, and she got lost. I found her after about a half hour.

"When we got home, she told my parents. She cried and they got angry at me. I was, well, I was at such an awful age. I felt put upon and resentful. So they sent me up to my room for a few hours. When it was time for us all to go to dinner, I was still sulking. And I...oh, Adam, I refused to go with them...and then, later that night, a policeman came to the door..."

"Shhh. It's okay. It's okay," Adam murmured soothingly as Leah, misty-eyed and tormented by memories, sank into his arms and nuzzled her face against him.

"This is awful," she muttered brokenly. "It was years ago. Verbena sent me to doctors, calmed my nightmares, everything. I don't usually go to pieces when I think about it, I swear I don't."

"I know," he murmured, stroking her hair. "But we've just spent a couple of hours knocking down all the usual barriers. A lot of things can come out of nowhere, surprising you like that."

She nodded. "I guess so."

He held her until she calmed down, then let her move to rest more comfortably at his side. "Verbena came out to Illinois, where we lived, right away," she said slowly, remembering. "I'm luckier than a lot of...orphans. There was never any question of 'whatever are we going to do with poor little Leah.' Even at a horrible age like that, and even after a terrible trauma like that, I could never doubt that she loved me and was happy I'd be living with her and Mordred. And she never tried to pretend that things were normal or that she could take my mother's place. I know she's not practical about most things, but nobody could have done a better job of helping me to recover."

"And Mordred?"

"He was great, too. When my parents were alive, we used to come here every Christmas and summer, since Verbena was just about our only relative. Mordred and I were always close. In a lot of ways, he took the place of my little sister."

"Really?" Adam murmured thoughtfully.

She nodded firmly. "I learned from my mistakes."

"What do you mean?"

"Well, I went through everything with the doctors, and I know I'm not to blame for my family's death. I mean, at first I thought I was somehow being punished. But they were hit head-on by a drunk driver on their way home from dinner, and my behavior had no influence on that. I guess you don't ever completely shake the guilt over something so awful, but at least I understand what's happening when I start to feel like it was all my fault.

"But the hardest thing to bear is that we were fighting the last time I saw them. The last thing I did before they died was to let all of them down, disappoint them, hurt them."

She gave a deep sigh. "That's a terrible thing to live with, Adam," she whispered.

"They loved you just as much when they—"

"I know. But I let them down. That was the last thing I did before they died. Nothing will ever change that. And I won't let it happen again."

Her voice was like steel, and he knew then that it was the creed she had lived by since recovering from her family's sudden death. Perhaps that resolution had even speeded her recovery, making her become more involved in the living— in Mordred and Verbena—than in her tragic memories.

She yawned sleepily and cuddled against him, exhausted by the torrent of emotions she had been through that night. He slid down against her and slung his leg over hers, feeling more protective toward her than he had ever felt in his life. He rubbed his cheek against her soft hair, his mind racing with thoughts.

He finally knew why Leah was always the perfect niece, the perfect cousin, the perfect acolyte. He finally understood why she felt so terribly responsible toward her family, why she picked up many more burdens than she needed to.

Apparently Mordred and Verbena couldn't or wouldn't or didn't even know they had to teach Leah that she wasn't personally responsible for keeping them safe and alive and happy.

Looking after Verbena's domestic problems was one thing, but how much would Leah's fiercely overprotective attitude in other matters affect the relationship that had blossomed between Leah and himself?

Physically exhausted as he was, he felt a lot of new worries nagging at his subconscious the rest of the night. He lay awake a long time, cherishing the feel of the woman in his arms and hoping this was more than an embarrassing mistake to her. When at last he drifted off, his sleep was troubled by confusing dreams. Consequently he was groggier than usual when Leah woke him the next morning.

"Adam. Adam, wake up," she whispered.

He grunted and settled more heavily on top of her, pinning her to the mattress. She wriggled beneath him.

"Adam," she said loudly.

"Hmm?"

She grasped his shoulders and tried to push him away. He obligingly rolled off her and to the other side of the bed. Leah rose to her knees and began shaking him in earnest. "Wake up!"

He flopped onto his back and opened his eyes. His look of bewilderment was comical.

"What are *you* doing here?" he asked earnestly.

She gave him a bland look and waited for him to remember. His gaze traveled down her disheveled hair to her naked body, and then to the tangled sheets and haphazardly discarded pillows lying around them.

After a moment, he clearly began to remember. "Wow," he said softly. Then he grinned and met her eyes. "Wow," he said more emphatically. "You're amazing. Bright, beautiful, *and* bawdy." He pulled her down into his arms and kissed her soundly.

"Hmm." She returned his kiss and wondered how they would ever get the day started.

"I feel very healthy this morning," he confided, and shifted position so she could feel just *how* healthy.

"What time is your plane?" she asked breathlessly a few minutes later, remembering the reason she had awoken him in the first place.

"What plane?" His hands curved around her bottom.

"The one you're taking to New York."

He frowned. Then the light started to dawn. "Oh, no. I'm going to New York today. What time is it?"

"Eight o'clock."

"In the morning?"

Leah looked out the window at the blazing sun and then back to Adam in exasperation. He sat up so suddenly she fell back against the mattress.

"Oh, no! My flight's at nine!"

"All right, calm down," she said, taking control of the situation. "You go take a shower. I'll finish packing for you."

"You?" he said doubtfully.

"Adam, if last night is anything to go by, a four-year-old child could pack a suitcase better than you."

He was still too sleepy to respond to the insult, so he slipped into the bathrobe she found for him. Just before leaving the room he glanced back at her and said hopefully, "Maybe we could shower together?"

She smiled. She liked being the object of his fantasies. "You'd never make your flight."

He sighed and went down the hall. Leah slipped into the shirt she had stripped off the night before and finished putting clothes and toiletries into his overnight bag. Then she went to her room to change and brush her hair. By the time she had finished making a pot of coffee in the kitchen, he was coming down the stairs.

"You're wearing that?" she said, putting a mug of coffee in front of him.

"Why not?" He was dressed in jeans and a white cotton shirt.

"I thought you wanted to look formidable for your publishers."

"Oh, that's not till tomorrow. Today I'm being interviewed by the *Times*."

"Oh."

Leah suddenly realized that for all the contempt he had received this summer from her and Melchior, and for all that Verbena treated him like an adoptive son, he was actually well-known and important in many circles.

She glanced at him again, thinking he would look somehow different now that she had remembered his position, but he was still the same Adam, ruggedly gorgeous, sleepy and cuddly, as he sipped his first cup of morning coffee. Only his eyes were different. They rested on her wherever she went in the kitchen, warm and intimate and full of reminders of the splendorous night they had shared together.

She refilled his mug. "Where's your ticket?"

"My pocket."

She glanced at the clock. "You'd better drink up. We should be going."

They drove to the airport in relative silence, both occupied with their own thoughts. When Leah parked the car near the terminal, he put his hand on her leg and said, "Don't come inside. An airport is a lousy place to talk."

"Okay." She covered his hand with hers and met his eyes. He looked restless.

"This is lousy timing."

Leah raised her brows.

"I mean, I wish I wasn't leaving today. Or I wish you could come with me."

"We're the only two people dumb enough to get stuck looking after the menagerie. One of us has to hold the fort."

He smiled and pulled her closer to kiss her lingeringly. She went to him willingly and answered him warmly. "I'll call you," he promised.

"Okay."

"And we have a lot to talk about when I get back."

"Yes." She didn't know what would happen, but suddenly, as far as her feelings about Adam were concerned, there was a lot more at stake than her aunt's good name. "I—"

"What?" he whispered encouragingly.

She sighed. "There's no point starting a conversation we haven't got time to finish."

He agreed reluctantly.

In place of promises she couldn't voice, she leaned forward and kissed him urgently. When their mouths parted, he touched her cheek, traced the delicate curve of her lower lip and let his hand drop down to massage a soft breast through the thin fabric of her summer blouse. She closed her eyes and rested her forehead against his shoulder.

Finally he pulled away. "You're a bad influence on me," he teased. "I haven't made out in a car since I was a teenager."

"I've *never* made out in a car," Leah said virtuously.

"When I get back, we'll park the car in the dark somewhere and go all the way together."

"Shouldn't they be calling your flight by now, Adam?" she said dryly, ignoring his leer.

He grinned, brushed another quick kiss across her lips and then hopped out of the car. As he swung his bag out of the back seat, Leah murmured, "Have a safe trip," in a voice gone suddenly tight and husky.

"Be nice to Ralu," he admonished and then walked off to catch his flight.

Ralu and Jenny appeared later in the day, armed with scented candles and some kind of incense that left an unbearable stench throughout the entire house.

The ferret escaped when they left. Leah chased him for an hour without success. Panting and sweating with exhaustion, she nearly gave up. Then a carload of Ithaca College summer students got stuck outside Verbena's house with engine trouble. They promised to help catch the ferret if Leah would give them all a ride back to campus after the car was towed.

It took considerable energy and determination, but they finally ensnared him. When Leah took hold of him, he curled up in her arms and regarded her innocently. She and the college kids trundled into the house, limp with fatigue. Adam wasn't kidding when he had said this sort of thing had really gotten him into shape.

After depositing her carload full of helpful students at their dorm, Leah treated herself to a gooey, sticky, fattening ice-cream sundae covered with nuts and hot fudge. Between a night in Adam's bed and a day in Verbena's house, she had no doubt that she had burned off enough calories in the past twenty-four hours to still come out ahead of the game.

Verbena called that afternoon to say Grimly had pulled through surgery with flying colors. The tumor was benign, and Grimly was already his old self, being rude and obstreperous and alienating the entire hospital staff. Verbena, however, planned to stay in England a little while longer, spoiling Grimly and doing research.

Adam called next. Leah recounted her day, adding, "And now the Questing Beast looks a little green around the gills."

"How can you tell?"

"His eyes are glassy, and he wouldn't eat the papaya I gave him. I wonder if Ralu's incense is having a bad effect on him."

"Did you mention this to Verbena? Maybe he's done this before."

"She's so relieved about Grimly, I didn't have the heart."

"No, I guess not. Maybe someone at Cornell University knows something about iguanas. Or is it iguannii?"

"I don't know. How is New York?"

"Hot, sticky, dirty, interesting. The usual."

"How did your interview go?"

"Oh, I was charming and impressive."

"And admirably modest, I'm sure," she added.

"That goes without saying."

"Well, have lots of fun in the Big Apple, because when you come home, I'm going to make you pay for all the work I'm doing alone now."

"And I'm going to make you pay for all those restless nights I had before last night."

Her voice was so soft he had trouble hearing it when she said, "I'll be waiting."

She was lost in a cloud when she hung up, and she continued to sit next to the phone, as if it could bring Adam closer to her. She pushed all doubts out of her mind for the moment and just enjoyed the thought of him. Doubts she would deal with when he got back.

The phone next to her rang again, startling her. She picked it up on the first ring. "Hello?"

"Miss McCargar?"

"Yes," she said.

"Where is your cousin?"

The abruptness of the question stunned her. "I don't know."

"We know he's been in touch with you, Leah."

The use of her name and the implied knowledge of her activities, voiced by a faceless stranger on the phone, frightened her.

"Who is this?" she demanded.

"When you see Mordred, tell him to turn himself in to us."

"I haven't—"

The stranger hung up. Leah put down the receiver very carefully. She picked up Chi, who was chewing on her shoelace, and held him on her lap, stroking him more for her own comfort than for his.

She didn't know what Mordred was involved in, but she had the distinct feeling she was out of her depth. She wondered if she should call the police. What could they do, though? So Mordred was flying down to Bolivia for some reason, and two strange men had called and urged her to tell him to turn himself over to them. She doubted the local sheriff could help her. After all, it wasn't as if she were being threatened.

She looked around the room nervously. How did they know Mordred had called her? Did they bug the phones? Did they watch her? And who were "they" anyhow?

She wished Adam were here. She had earlier refused to betray Mordred's trust to him, but now she felt afraid. She would feel so much safer if he were there to listen to her fragmented story, to investigate mysterious sounds in the night, to hold and comfort her, to make love to her. . . .

Taking hold of her usual strength of will, she reminded herself that the house was full of animals. It was little comfort to realize that T'ai and Chi would undoubtedly welcome Jack the Ripper himself into the house, the ferret was nothing but a nuisance, the mynah bird was half-mad and the Questing Beast was silent and afraid of strangers.

Macbeth came over to slobber on her skirt and beg for dog biscuits. She gave him a big hug. "At least you're fairly normal. I can count on you, can't I?"

She was too tired and nervous to deal with the water bed tonight. After checking one last time on all the food and water bowls, she went up to Adam's room and tumbled into his bed. She didn't think he would mind at all.

The mattress was firm and comfortable, and the crisp sheets bore his musky scent. She hugged her pillow, closed her eyes and inhaled the delicious essence of the man. Her man. Her eyes flew open in surprise as the words entered her mind unbidden. She looked around the darkened room and let last night's scene replay in her mind again and again. Lulled by the memory, she finally fell into a restless, dream-filled sleep.

The next day was worse than the one before. It was cloudy all morning, and by afternoon the heaviness of the coming storm was making Leah feel lethargic and cranky. Ralu's chanting rose to new heights of amplitude, and Leah had a pounding headache by the time the woman left.

She took the Questing Beast to the university and found that his illness wasn't that specialized, after all. He had eaten a button. The staff applied a ruthless solution to the problem and told Leah it was free of charge; how often did they get to diagnose an iguana, after all? He looked much perkier as they drove home, although Leah drew some peculiar stares as she rode through town with a dragon on a dog leash at her side.

It began pouring down rain when they reached Verbena's house. Thunder and lightning followed, adding to the ache in Leah's head that the aspirin she had taken couldn't seem to alleviate.

"Stress," she said wearily. "Stress." She would be better off spending next year's summer vacation in Beirut.

She fed the animals, plucked weeds and burrs out of their fur, cooked dinner, cleaned the kitchen and then finally sat down to do some work on her thesis.

There was a mighty crash of thunder and the lights went out.

"Oh, that's just great," she muttered. She tried to remember where they used to keep the candles. The lights in Verbena's rustic house often failed during storms.

There was another clap of thunder, and Macbeth let out a bloodcurdling howl. He, T'ai, Chi and the Questing Beast all cowered nervously at Leah's feet. King John and the ever-growing number of cats prowled restlessly around the house, tense and jumpy from the clatter of rain beating against the windows, the sudden flashes of lightning in the stormy sky and the unearthly thunder that seemed to shake the floorboards.

The phone rang.

Leah stared at it, feeling unreasonably frightened. She was surprised that it even worked, now that the lights had gone out. Or had they really gone out? Could someone have cut the power lines?

"Oh, for God's sake, Leah," she scolded herself. So it was a dark and stormy night. So what? Verbena loved storms. She, Leah and Mordred used to sit by the window and watch the impressive sight of clouds speeding across the angry sky.

The phone continued ringing. Leah chided herself sternly as she moved forward to pick it up. As soon as she picked up the receiver and spoke into it, the line went dead.

She couldn't have said why, but that struck her as more sinister than the anonymous phone calls. Was someone trying to determine if she was home?

"Candles. I've got to get candles," she said hoarsely.

The dogs hung at her feet, impeding her steps and tripping her repeatedly as she searched the house. She was too grateful for their company to mind. She couldn't find candles in any of the usual places. Becoming desperate, she remembered that Jenny and Ralu had left some of their candles in Xanadu, the haunted room.

Since a hostile spiritual presence was the least of Leah's fears at the moment, she ran all the way up to the third floor, pursued closely by mammal and reptile alike. When she found the remains of Ralu's horrendously scented candles, she remembered that she hadn't brought any matches with her. Cursing with annoyance, she took four candles in hand and descended the stairs in the dark, tripping over furry bodies the whole way.

There were definitely matches in the kitchen, she thought, making her way though the dark house in that direction.

Lightning flashed across the sky again, casting eerie shadows in her path. She nearly gibbered as an insubstantial form appeared before her. In the next moment it was gone, a fleeting jest of the storm. Thunder crashed overhead, and the rain beat harder against the windows.

As she approached the kitchen, she stopped abruptly. Something was wrong. Her common sense warred with her jangled nerves for a moment as she tried to determine what was bothering her.

Suddenly Macbeth stopped cowering in a seemingly boneless huddle at her feet. He crept in front of her with predatory stealth, his eyes glued to the broad wooden door leading to the kitchen.

The door. She had left it open and now it was closed. Her heart started pounding.

Think, she ordered herself. Could it have closed by itself? Could an animal have brushed it closed? Are you *sure* you left it open?

Macbeth rose to his full height. For the first time in her memory, Leah heard him growl. That frightened her most of all.

Then she heard it, too. The unmistakable sound of someone in the kitchen, rifling through drawers and cabinets. It was a horrible, furtive noise. Threatening. Deadly.

They kept knives in the kitchen.

Her stomach churned. She wanted to cry. She wanted to run screaming out the front door. She didn't understand why her stubborn nature insisted on protecting Verbena's house and menagerie.

Trembling with fear and blazing with anger against the intruder, Leah looked around for a defensive weapon. Her hands seized upon a heavy brass candelabra. She had always hated it anyhow, so she could be reckless with it if necessary.

She crept silently toward the door, toward her enemy, with the candelabra clutched between her arms. Macbeth's growl grew in intensity. The Shih Tzus sniffed at the door.

Suddenly the scuffling noises inside the kitchen came to an abrupt halt. Whoever he was, he suspected they were there. They must make their move now.

Accompanied by Macbeth's barking and a mighty blast of thunder, Leah burst through the swinging door with a shriek, her long hair flying and her arms raised over her head as she brandished the brass candelabra.

The intruder screamed and fell back against the far wall. His flailing arms knocked over porcelain pots of flour, sugar and rice. The clatter was deafening as they shattered on the floor.

Macbeth ran through the dark room. He jumped on top of the intruder, but instead of drawing blood, he began sniffing him curiously.

Leah rushed across the room, not quite sure what she meant to do.

"No! Don't!" screamed the intruder. Using the belly-up method of defense, he sank to the flour-sugar-rice-covered floor and covered his head with his hands.

Leah gasped in astonishment as she recognized the voice, the movement and the posture.

Lightning flashed into the room, illuminating his terror-stricken expression as he risked a peek up at her.

He scowled suddenly.

"What the bloody hell are you doing? You look like the madwoman in *Jane Eyre*!" he snapped.

"Mordred?" she croaked an instant before her legs gave way, and she sank gracelessly to the floor.

Nine

Leah sat in a limp heap, drawing gulps of air and gaping at her cousin. Slim, dark haired and dark eyed like Leah, Mordred looked thin, unkempt, wet, exhausted and alarmingly pale. The pallor, Leah realized, could possibly be attributed to the flour and sugar that covered him in a thin, uneven layer. She started laughing.

"What's so funny?" he demanded. "Don't get hysterical, Leah. We haven't got time for hysterics."

That sobered her. "What are you doing sneaking around here in the dark?" she snapped.

"The lights won't go on," he said impatiently. "And I was sneaking around, as you put it, to avoid attracting Mother's menagerie while I looked for candles." Macbeth had finally recognized Mordred and was now whining and pawing at him in an effort to inspire an affectionate greeting. "Can't you get this beast away from me?" Mordred pleaded.

"You would think—"

"Arrgh! What the blue blazes is that?" Mordred cried.

Leah glanced over her shoulder. "Oh. That's the Questing Beast."

"It looks like a big iguana!"

"It is."

"Leah, in heaven's name, can't you keep Mother under control? Surely even she must realize—"

"Why aren't you in Bolivia?" Leah interrupted as she pushed herself into a standing position.

"I never intended to go to Bolivia. I don't know anyone there. I don't even speak Spanish. And I hear the climate is appalling."

Leah rolled her eyes heavenward, then went to pull Macbeth off Mordred and help Mordred stand up. The two cousins regarded each other wearily for a moment and then embraced. "Here. Sit on a chair while I light these candles," Leah said at last. "Why on earth did you tell me you were going to Bolivia?"

"Well, I had previously told you I was coming home, even though I didn't want anyone to know that. Then it occurred to me they might be bugging your phone, so obviously I had to mislead them."

Having lit two candles, Leah slid into a chair across from Mordred. "Who are 'they'?"

He shrugged helplessly. "I'm not quite sure. CIA, FBI, the National Guard, several large metropolitan police departments, the National Defense Agency, a few ill-mannered private eyes—"

"Mordred! What have you *done*?"

"I'm not actually sure. I was using my computer modem to hunt for some information my company needed. I stumbled across a top-secret security system and—just out of curiosity, just for a purely intellectual exercise, I swear—I broke into it."

"You broke into someone's secret computer files?" Leah repeated in horror. "Whose?"

"That's the trouble! I don't know. But whoever they are, they're not regarding this in the harmless way I intended it." He clearly felt *he* was the injured party.

"How did they find you?"

"It wouldn't be that difficult. And...well, the system was so interesting I explored it several times. I suppose it was my repeated breach of their security that really infuriated them."

"Did they threaten you?"

"Four large, humorless men with bad tailors and nasty-looking weapons tucked into their suit coats showed up at my apartment, saying they would like to talk to me. I cleverly escaped." He waited expectantly, but when Leah didn't rise to the bait, he sighed and continued, "They staked out my apartment. A day later some very similar men showed up at my girlfriend's house. By the end of the week, everyone I knew and every place I could go had become unsafe for me."

"So you decided to come home, but you wanted everyone to think you weren't coming here." She gasped and clutched his arm.

Mordred jumped out of his chair. "What! What?"

"They know you're here! The phone rang earlier. The line went dead when I—"

"That was me. I wanted to make sure you were home, but I couldn't speak in case they were listening."

"You scared me! I've been getting strange phone calls. Men who want to contact you. Men who want you to turn yourself in to them. Oh, Mordred! You're really in big trouble this time."

"You've got to hide me," he said emphatically.

"No, I can't! Mordred, these are the police! Or something like that. You've got to turn yourself in to them. Surely you can explain—"

"*Explain?* Oh, Leah, Leah, you're so naive. They'll lock me up and throw away the key. *After* they torture and brainwash me. Don't you understand? Didn't you see *Three Days of the Condor*?''

The more she insisted he give himself up to the authorities, the more hysterical he became. Finally Leah relented. She would hide him for a few days, and once he had had enough rest and enough to eat, she hoped he would see reason when they discussed it again.

"I just want to curl up in my own bed," he moaned at last.

That made Leah gasp again. "Adam! You can't stay in the house, Adam will be back from New York tomorrow."

"Who the devil is Adam?"

"He's Verbena's collaborator. He's staying here, in my old room."

"Is Mother in New York, too?"

"No, London. Mordred . . . I'm sorry to have to tell you that Grimly has been ill, although he's getting better."

Mordred stared at her for a moment and then shook his head. "I'm very sorry for Mother's sake, but in all honesty, despite the man's biological relationship to me, we hardly know each other and we've never particularly liked each other."

Leah nodded in understanding. There was no point in saying more. He certainly wasn't in any position to fly over to London to comfort Verbena. "In any event, you can't stay in your old room. Or anywhere on the second floor. Adam would notice you immediately."

"All right, forget the second floor. I'll hide in Xanadu. No one ever goes up there."

"You can't." She explained about Jenny Harper, Ralu and their hostile spiritual friend. "They're there every day."

"You can't be serious," Mordred said.

"I swear to you it's true."

"How about the cellar?"

"No. What will happen if Adam goes down there without warning to haul up more cracked corn or dog meal?"

"Maybe I should just get out of your way and go stay with strangers," Mordred said grumpily.

"The shed! The one out back that we used to use as a fort when we were kids."

"Is that thing still standing?"

"Yes. Adam even said there were some blankets in there."

"And probably mice, rats, snakes and raccoons, too. Forget it. No way. Absolutely not."

As soon as the rain subsided they carried blankets, pillows, food, candles, matches and other necessities out to the shed at the back of Verbena's property. Mordred grumbled and cursed and complained, but he was asleep before Leah had even finished tidying up.

She passed a restless night, tossing and turning and worrying. Not only was she probably breaking the law by helping Mordred, even temporarily, but she was perhaps also compromising Verbena, since she was hiding him on Verbena's property. Worst of all, how would she keep this from Adam? He wasn't nearly as obtuse as her aunt. Quite the opposite, in fact. Her only hope was to convince Mordred to turn himself in before Adam discovered his presence.

She overslept the next morning. Since she now had Mordred to take care of in addition to the menagerie, she ran well behind schedule the rest of the day. Consequently she was late in picking Adam up at the airport that afternoon. He was waiting outside the terminal when she pulled the car up. Typically cheerful, he grinned and waved when he saw her, hopped into the car and pulled her close for an affectionate hug and quick kiss.

"How'd everything go without me?" he asked.

"Oh, just fine," she lied, wondering if lightning would strike her. Nothing happened. Apparently the furies forgave lying in a good cause.

"Miss me?" he persisted.

"How did things go in New York?" she asked instead.

"Great." He didn't elaborate. Lavish Books had made a substantial offer on *Licentious Nuns*, but he knew better than to think Leah would be pleased about that.

She told him about the menagerie and about the storm, saying that the electricity had been restored that morning. He told her about the *Times* interview and some research he'd had the chance to do. They said a lot of nothing.

They had company when they got home. Two large, humorless men with bad tailors sat in a dark four-door car in Verbena's driveway. Leah's heart started pounding. The men got out of their car at the same moment Leah and Adam got out of theirs. Did she imagine it, or did nasty weapons bulge under the arms of their suit coats?

Adam glanced over at Leah. She looked as white as a sheet, he thought with alarm. She wet her lips twice and tilted her head, but she seemed incapable of speech.

"Can we help you?" Adam said to the two men at last. They looked like Hollywood's idea of FBI agents.

"RMQE, sir," said one of the men. "Special Attachment, Security and Intelligence."

Since Leah still said nothing, Adam made the introductions.

"Miss McCargar, we're looking for your cousin, Mordred McCargar. We have reason to believe—"

"He's in Bolivia, isn't he?" Leah said with unconvincing casualness.

"No, he's not, Miss McCargar. We have reason to believe he may try to contact you." The two men simultaneously raised their brows in silent inquiry.

"No, no, you're mistaken. Mordred told me he's not coming home after all."

Adam listened dumbfounded as the interview continued for several minutes. Since Leah clearly didn't want to invite these men into the house, they all stood out in the driveway together. The two men persisted in trying to determine if Mordred had called or seen Leah. Leah, looking as if she might be ill at any moment, continued to deny it.

"If you should see him," said the taller of the two men at last, "if he does happen to call or stop by, please ask him to call me at this number. He's in serious trouble, Miss Mc-Cargar, and he would be very wise to stop running away."

Leah took the card, but didn't respond. She felt frightened for Mordred, who cowered in an abandoned shed at this very moment, and horrified at herself for willingly lying to the authorities.

She watched with relief as the two men got in their car and drove away. The relief was short-lived. Adam's speculative gaze seemed to burn straight through her when she met his eyes.

She turned quickly and went to the house. He followed right behind her. She had barely closed the front door when he said, "All right. What's going on?"

"I don't know," she said, continuing to walk away from him. "Mordred seems to be in some kind of trouble."

"Come on, Leah. You looked like you were about to faint when they got out of the car. You know more than you're letting on," he insisted, following her into the kitchen.

"Hungry?" she asked. "No, I guess it's a bit early for dinner. Maybe some iced tea? You look—"

"Leah!" He grabbed her arms and pulled her forward. Seeing the panic in her eyes, he relented. Instead of releasing her, however, he folded his arms tightly around her and pulled her against his chest. He laid his cheek against her hair and gave a deep sigh. "Can't you trust me? I know that you know more about Mordred than you're telling me. Do you have to carry the burden alone? Do his problems have to weigh so heavily on you?"

The sympathy in his voice, the strength in his arms and the comfort of his embrace wore away at Leah's resolve. She rested her cheek against his shoulder and slid her arms around his back. Finally she said, "I know more than I've told you, that's true. But I swore to Mordred I would say nothing until . . . he said otherwise."

Leah's loyalty to her family was everything to her, but it wasn't enough for Adam. He didn't want Mordred's problems to tear her apart like this, any more than he wanted her to let her concern for Verbena come between them.

He couldn't do anything about Mordred, but maybe he could do something about the other problem, he thought, coming to a sudden decision.

"We need to talk," he said.

Leah didn't think she could take any more trauma that day, but Adam was right. They did need to talk. She straightened her shoulders and agreed.

"Let's go sit in the sun," he suggested. "It's a beautiful day."

Leah made two big glasses of iced tea, and they sat in a patch of grass in the partial shadow of a tree.

"Lavish Books made a generous offer," Adam told her. "More generous than I think Verbena will be able to get from her usual publisher. Whether or not she kicks me off the project, I'm going to recommend to her that she go ahead with Lavish."

He waited for Leah to explode. He was surprised, even a little concerned, when she simply stared off into the distance instead.

Finally she nodded. Then she shrugged and said uncomfortably, "You have to tell her about your degree, of course. I couldn't let you— It just wouldn't be right, Adam." She lowered her head and added huskily, so softly that he barely heard her, "I wish I didn't know. I wish Melchior hadn't told me."

His heart swelled, and he felt incredibly tender toward her. Somewhere along the way, and probably against her will, she had encompassed him in that small circle of people to whom she gave her unswerving loyalty. Her feelings even overrode her conviction that he had been thoroughly dishonest with Verbena. And the paradox, he realized, was wearing away at her conscience.

"Oh, Leah," he murmured. She raised tear-filled eyes to him, and his arms went around her. Without conscious thought, his lips covered hers and he pressed her back into the grass. Lost in the honeyed taste of her kiss, he forgot what he had intended to tell her.

Their mouths moved together hungrily, and they clung to each other in desperation. He had lain awake for two nights in New York remembering every moment of the night Leah had spent in his arms, wondering if she would come to him again when he returned, or turn away from him.

Her words had confirmed that she cared about him, and the restless movements of her hips underneath his confirmed that she had endured the same enticing, merciless and erotic dreams that he had had for the past two nights.

His hands slid longingly over her body, massaging her heaving breasts, teasing her erect nipples, smoothing across her flat belly and sliding down her thighs. He fumbled for the hem of her cotton sundress and slid one hand underneath to stroke her legs.

"Soft, you're so soft," he whispered against her lips. "Two days. I missed you like I was starving to death."

"So did I," she admitted breathlessly, pressing her open mouth against his neck and tugging his shirt out of his jeans.

He stroked his way up her thighs. He touched her lacy panties and cupped his hand over the soft, damp heat he could feel there. They looked into each other's eyes.

"I want you," he whispered.

He flattened his palm against her and moved it in a firm rhythmic motion, back and forth, gently rubbing and teasing. Primitive instinct seized Leah, robbing her of thought or will. She moaned repeatedly, and moved her hips against his teasing hand. She tore at his clothes, pushing his shirt aside so she could touch him, fumbling ineffectually at his belt.

"Look at me," he insisted when her eyes closed.

She forced her heavy lids open, and the passion in his blue gaze stole her breath. Their eyes held as he pushed her underpants down her legs. She felt the touch of his warm fingers against that most intimate of places, felt them slide through her crisply curling hair and then delve into her hot, wet, sensitive flesh.

"Yes, yes, oh, Adam, yes," she murmured over and over, scarcely aware of what she was saying.

She squeezed her eyes shut and clutched his shirt. Her hips moved in frantic, mindless response to his coaxing. He whispered into her ear, and the things he said added sharp images and hot longing to the urgent need sweeping through her body. His caress became more insistent, his strokes faster, his touch bolder.

"Ohh," she cried at last as fire coursed through her. She could hear his voice murmuring softly. She could feel his body as the only solid thing in a swirling universe. Her arms slid around him gratefully as she sank back to earth. She felt the strength in the smooth back under her palms, the toughness of the arms that held her, the gentleness of the lips that brushed across her neck and face, and she knew that at last, at last she had found someone who could shelter her.

Leah opened her eyes. He was looking down at her. His face was so full of tenderness and desire, she could never feel embarrassed that he had watched her in such an abandoned and vulnerable moment.

He lowered his head, and they kissed again, long and sweetly, tongues dueling and caressing, both of them eagerly acknowledging how special this all was.

He spread increasingly demanding kisses over her face, neck and shoulders while she unbuckled his belt. Her trembling hands unsnapped his jeans and then, ever so gently, she unzipped them and freed him from their constraint.

"What a relief," he murmured, and she smiled.

He helped her push his jeans down just far enough for their purpose, and then he rolled onto his back, pulling her on top of him. "This isn't a nice soft bed," he replied to her questioning look.

She knelt above him. Holding her eyes, he led her hand to his throbbing masculine heat and folded his fingers around hers.

"Mmm," Leah sighed. "There's more to you than meets the eye."

"I'm full of surprises," he said modestly.

"I've noticed."

"It's about time."

"Oh, I noticed all along."

"Really?"

She nodded. She tightened her fist around him. He drew in a sharp breath.

"It's all yours," he said huskily, releasing her fingers and settling his hands on her thighs.

They watched each other with fascination as she slid down onto him, slowly and gracefully, moving as his hands guided her.

With Leah's skirt spread around them and their hands moving freely over each other's bodies, they ground their hips together in a slow, undulating motion that spun out their pleasure a long, long time. Sweat glistened on Adam's face and ran between Leah's breasts. Her thighs burned beneath his stroking palms. His chest was hot and damp wherever she touched it.

Their breath grew so rapid and frantic they could no longer whisper to each other. Sheer sensation became so overwhelming that Leah closed her eyes and tilted her head back, pushing harder against his forceful thrusts.

They melted against each other simultaneously. Leah felt tears streak down her face as she collapsed against him, trembling in the wake of the most soul-searing pleasure she had ever known. She pillowed her head against Adam's chest, which was heaving with his harsh, labored breath. His arms squeezed her so tightly she couldn't get enough air, but she didn't mind.

She heard him murmur her name with something like awe in his voice, and then his mouth moved roughly against her hair. Limp and damp, shattered with stunning pleasure, raw emotion and sheer exhaustion, they clung together until sleep claimed them both.

"Hey, wake up." Adam's whisper and the gentle pressure of his hands on Leah's shoulders roused her several hours later. She opened her eyes. He was lying beneath her in the grass and smiling at her with an expression that made her heart turn over. Then she noticed how dark it was.

"Gosh, what time is it?" she murmured sleepily.

"I don't know." He glanced at the fading light in the western sky. "Between eight and nine, maybe?"

"Good grief!" She sat up suddenly. She reached for her underwear and pulled it on as she spoke, straightening her dress and smoothing her hair. "T'ai and Chi will chew the house to pieces if we don't feed them right away. And the Questing Beast was supposed to have his medicine two hours ago."

"Duty, duty, duty." Adam stood, adjusted his clothing and stretched. "I feel great! And I'm starving." He glanced at her hopefully. "I don't suppose you'd like to make dinner tonight?"

"Do you want to catch the Questing Beast and give him his medicine?" she asked archly.

They haggled over their list of chores. Adam finally decided that making dinner was the easiest task and relented. Leah was feeding the dogs when Adam came out onto the back porch and said, "Dinner will be ready in about an hour."

"What are we having?"

"Pizza."

She scowled at him. "That's cheating. I expected to see you laboring over a hot stove."

"I even bribed them to deliver it."

"They don't usually like to come this far out of town," Leah agreed, setting down the food bowls.

Adam came up behind her and slid his arms around her. "And an hour..."

"Hmm?" She felt her pulse accelerate when he pressed a moist kiss against her neck.

"Should be just enough time..." He slid his hands over her belly.

"Yes?"

"For us to shower." He pressed his hips against her bottom.

She glanced up at him. "You want to wash? Now?"

"You'll wash me, I'll wash you. It'll be fun."

She pretended to be skeptical.

"Come on. Humor me," he said, taking her hand and leading her back inside the house.

It *was* fun.

Under the hot, refreshing shower spray, they lathered each other's bodies with elaborate thoroughness. Long after they were clean and the water had turned tepid, they continued to play together. And that's just what it was, Leah thought with wonder—playing. Adam's happy, teasing nature released something in her that she had kept bottled up and buried under responsibility since her childhood. It was a release as profoundly gratifying as the sexual release she had experienced earlier in his arms.

They finally got cold enough to cease their games and go to their rooms to find their robes. Wearing his bathrobe, Adam entered Leah's bedroom without knocking. He dried her hair, then threw the towel over her head, pushed her back onto the sloshing water bed and tickled her while she tried to untangle herself. They both laughed and began wrestling with such exuberance that they eventually rolled off the bed and slid down to the floor.

"I win!" Adam declared with satisfaction, straddling her body and pinning her shoulders to the floor.

"That was a sneak attack," Leah accused.

"Go tell it to the referee." His eyes gleamed. "Now the question is, what's my reward?"

"You have a lot of gall to expect a reward for attacking me in my own room."

"I'll make it up to you. You can attack me in my room later. In fact, I'd prefer it if you did. Your bed is *awful*." He reached down to her prostrate body and started to pull apart the neckline of her bathrobe. "I say winner takes all."

"You would." She met his lips as he bent forward to press a gentle kiss to her mouth. Her arms slid around his neck to hold him there. She gazed into his eyes, adoring him.

"What are you thinking?" he whispered.

She shrugged. "That you're good for me." She smiled. "And that you give a whole new meaning to soap and water."

"I'm starting to think you're pretty good for me, too," he murmured. He slid down along her body and pressed his hips against hers so she could feel the effect she had on him. "You're a little physically taxing, but otherwise I think you're just what the doctor ordered."

The word "doctor" reminded him of what he wanted to tell her. Torn between the desire to talk to her and the desire to make love to her again, he was trying to make up his mind when they heard the front doorbell ring.

"There's dinner," murmured Leah.

"Yeah." He stayed on top of her, lost in her dark, tender eyes.

"Maybe I should get it," she said at last. "And you," she said significantly, "should probably try to calm down."

"Spoilsport," he chided as she pushed him away and rose to her feet.

"Where's your wallet? *Buying* dinner was, after all, your idea, and I'm only a poor grad student."

"On my dresser."

Leah straightened her robe and walked out. Her hair was mussed, her robe was wrinkled and her lips were swollen, but she didn't seem to notice. Adam grinned. He liked seeing her when she wasn't perfect. He loved it, in fact.

He stood, straightened his robe and went to stand by the window. Leah's room had an excellent view of the backyard. He frowned. Was that the flare of a match out in the woods? He continued to stare, but there was no further sign of anything unusual. After a moment he shrugged and dismissed the thought. Perhaps it was a lightning bug—or simply his imagination.

He looked up at the star-filled sky. Another beautiful night, he thought. He hoped Leah would spend the rest of it with him. He was about to bring up a subject of controversy between them. He wondered if it would shift her loyalty, and consequently her affection, away from him again. He hoped she would understand, but if she didn't, then there really was no hope for them. She would never be able to respect him. It was better to know now, before he got in too deep.

The knowledge that he was already in too deep weighed on him like a granite boulder as he went downstairs to the kitchen.

Ten

"What do you want to drink?" Leah asked as Adam entered the kitchen. She had already set everything out and was unwrapping the pizza. "You ordered it just the way I like it. How did you know?"

He sat at his place and watched as she poured iced tea into his glass and put a piece of pizza before him. He stared at it, his mind working as he tried to organize his thoughts.

"What's wrong?" Leah asked at last.

He took a deep breath. "I'm not hungry."

"An hour ago you said you were starved."

"I . . . We have to talk." She looked blank. "I wanted to tell you this afternoon, but then we…got distracted. I have a hell of a time concentrating around you."

Realizing he was very serious, Leah put her fork down and gave him her full attention. "Well?"

"It's about what happened at Barrington University."

Leah shifted uncomfortably and lowered her eyes. "I'm sorry I was so awful about that, Adam, but you must realize how this could affect—"

"I know, I know. But frankly, at the moment I'm more concerned with how it will affect us." That got her attention. "I think Verbena will forgive my trespasses against her more easily than you will. And it's your understanding that's coming to mean the most to me."

The quiet force of his words made emotion well up inside her: the need to be loved, to be protected, to share intimacy. Above all, she needed to believe in him. She hoped with every part of her soul that he was about to tell her something she could forgive. "Go on," she said huskily.

"I got into Barrington because I honestly deserved to. I had terrific grades at Cornell and excellent recommendations. I did well at Barrington, too, but I clashed too much with some of the faculty there. They were prestigious and established, but they were also unimaginative, cautious and inflexible.

"I know that you and I differ on how history should be presented in books," he added defensively, "but I believe in my work just as much as you believe in yours."

"I guess I should have known that a long time ago," Leah said softly. Whatever she might think of pop historians, Adam was sincere and honest. He was no slick, irresponsible opportunist.

"So when I came up with a topic for my thesis, I was very enthusiastic about it. Melchior Browning was my adviser. It took me a while to convince him that my topic was valid and interesting, and that I could find enough reliable sources. But I did."

"What happened?" Leah asked.

"We didn't get along at all. I thought his advice was useless and uninspired. I thought he personally was pompous and condescending. The only person on the staff I would have liked to have had as my adviser instead was on sabbatical my final year. So I wound up just going my own way. I scarcely met with Melchior at all the last eight months I worked on my thesis.

"I finished all my course work. I passed all my final doctoral exams with flying colors. All that was left was to present and defend my dissertation."

Bitterness clouded his face as he recalled those final weeks at Barrington University. "Melchior looked it over briefly and refused to let me present it. He hated it. He urged me to start all over, closely following his guidance this time."

"Why did he hate it so much?"

Adam shrugged. "He gave me a lot of reasons. The same reasons he probably repeated to you. With all due modesty, I think he hated it because it was original, daring, well written, accessible and interesting. Everything that history, in Melchior's eyes, shouldn't be."

"What did you do?" Leah asked. She couldn't even imagine the despair she would feel if her adviser told her her thesis shouldn't be presented.

"I absolutely refused to be his acolyte. That was the best work I was capable of, I believed in it, I stood behind it. I demanded my right to present it. He tried to block me. It was a stalemate for weeks."

"And you quit?" Leah asked. It didn't seem like him to simply give up.

"I was called before a meeting of the full professors in the department and a few big-shot university administrators. They decided to have an inquiry. An inquiry!" He threw his hands up, still exasperated after all these years. "The subject of my thesis simply stopped being the issue. All of a sudden I was immersed in a ridiculous controversy about power plays in the academic world. No one even cared about what I had written anymore. They were just upset that a promising grad student was rebelling."

"So you walked out?"

He nodded. "After a few more useless meetings in which everyone even refused to look at my work until we had settled the issue. To me, the work *was* the issue."

He looked terribly sad as he said, "I had wanted to be a history professor since I was seventeen. I admired scholars like your aunt the way most boys admire football stars. I wanted to be part of the dusty books, fascinating research, hard-won grants, enthusiastic students, squeaky chalkboards, ivy-covered campuses..."

He shrugged. "That's what I always thought my life would be. But I was a grown man when they did this to my work, and I knew that I couldn't live with the ridiculous hypocrisy, childish power plays and vicious back stabbing. Maybe if it happened now I'd stick it out to the bitter end, but I was younger and less tolerant then."

"So since you had completed all the other work successfully, and had written your thesis but been denied the right to present it, you felt yourself entitled to the doctorate anyhow," Leah said softly.

He shook his head and said emphatically, "No. Absolutely not. When I walked away from Barrington, I washed my hands of the academic world for good."

"I don't understand how you...why Verbena..."

"Well, since I had suddenly changed my life plan, and I didn't even have a Ph.D. to show for all those years I spent in school, I started looking around pretty quickly for a way to live. I had taken time off before to work in construction, and I did that again while I tried to sort out my life."

That must be where his impressive muscles came from, Leah thought.

"I had an old friend who worked in a publishing house in New York. She was the one who suggested I submit my work as nonfiction to the editors there."

"And that's how you first got published?"

"Yes. Of course, it helped to have a friend on the inside. Even so, the book did really well when it came out. Much better than everyone expected. So when I started writing *Reach for the Scepter*, Lavish Books made a huge offer on it. More money than I ever thought I would earn, to be honest."

He gave her a humorless, cynical smile. "And suddenly Melchior and the other great minds at Barrington realized that I was going to be very well known, and that I could easily make them look ridiculous for alienating this 'brilliant young historical writer' that everyone suddenly wanted to interview, hire for consultation or invite to be a guest speaker.

"So Melchior and his cronies swallowed their pride and very, very quietly awarded me an honorary Ph.D. to make up for the one they had denied me—the one I had earned."

"Oh my goodness," Leah said in a low voice. She knew things like that happened. Verbena had occasionally repeated such tales to her, full of disgust that her colleagues weren't above being narrow-minded or self-serving.

"I was tempted to tell them in graphic detail what they could do with their phony degree. But, well, it meant a lot to my parents. My dad is a welder, my brother works in construction, too, and my sister is a dancer. I was the only one in our family to go to college. They were really proud of me, and they did a lot to help me get by financially. My mom always wanted to say, 'My son, the doctor.' They thought I had a right to the degree, and I thought *they* had a right to it. So I took it. But Melchior Browning is the only person in the world I let call me *Dr.* Jordan. And with him, I insist."

"I think I've lost my appetite." Leah pushed her plate away. She was silent for a long time, thinking. Suddenly she made an inarticulate sound of fury. Adam's eyes widened when she struck the table with her fist.

"You're that mad?" he asked weakly.

"Filthy hypocrite! I can't believe it!"

"Who?" Adam asked in confusion.

"Melchior! I was disgusted before, but now, knowing that he ruined your chances for your doctorate, then tried to bribe you into silence with an honorary degree, and then had the utter, unmitigated gall to 'confide' in me about your 'deception'—ooh, it makes me want to throttle the man!"

She looked like she would do it, too. Adam laughed with delight. That drew Leah's startled gaze to his face. He took her fist and smoothed the tense fingers between his hands.

"My champion," he murmured.

"Oh, Adam, I feel just terrible," she said morosely.

"Well, you did have a point. I really did quit my doctoral program just before they threw me out, Leah. I didn't earn the degree they gave me. It was a bribe, just as you said." He frowned. "They just assumed I had so little character I would publicly rant and rave about their unfairness every time I had the chance."

"The one thing I don't understand is why you didn't tell Verbena."

"It's not really part of my life, Leah. It didn't seem important at first. I knew my Barrington degree wasn't why she had chosen me. It was only after we started working together and I had much more contact than usual with other professors—her colleagues—that I remembered how important that kind of thing is in her world. To be honest, I meant to tell her. Things were just so chaotic, and then Melchior told that story at lunch that day to get under my skin about the college professor who had phony credentials.... It upset Verbena so much, I didn't know how to bring it up after that. And it made me resentful, too."

"I don't mean this the way it sounds, Adam, but why *did* Verbena choose you?"

He smiled briefly. "That's a lot milder than most of your questions have been. I guess she asked me because she needs me."

Leah's face showed her disbelief.

"It's true," he said quietly. "She's a great teacher, a fabulous researcher, a wonderful woman and a brilliant scholar, but she writes even worse than she cooks. Her last book was a mighty flop. Even most scholars couldn't make head or tail of her prose. It was so convoluted that even her accuracy came into question. She needs a good writer working with her. And she's getting older, Leah. She needs somebody who can spark off ideas with her, who can suggest other sources.''

''I guess so,'' Leah said uncomfortably. The idea that Verbena was getting old bothered her.

They were silent for a while. At last Adam said, ''You're taking this awfully well. About me, I mean.''

''Did you really think I would look down my nose at you?''

''You have so far,'' he pointed out quietly. He was still feeling the pain of her contempt. He could easily brush off slights from everyone except her.

''I know,'' she said contritely. Her dark eyes misted over. ''I grew up in that world you're talking about, the one you walked away from. Before I came to live with Verbena, I idolized her for her brilliance. After I moved in and realized she was, well, negligent about practical things, I still admired her and I wanted to be a professor and scholar, too.'' She spread her hands. ''You're so different, your attitudes are so different. I was taught to think writers like you were irreverent and careless and polluted the field.''

''Writers like *what*? You admitted you've never even read a word I've written. You're condemning me on vague hearsay and general prejudice.'' His voice was angrier then he had intended.

His words stung. Primarily because they were true. She lowered her head. ''That's *true*, and it does me no credit that I've only changed my mind because . . .''

''Why?'' he persisted.

She ignored his probing gaze and said, ''My main concern is that no one, including you, hurts Verbena or her reputation.''

''Don't you think after nearly forty years in the field Verbena can look after her own reputation?''

''You know she's fond of you personally, Adam. I was afraid she might allow her feelings to influence her decisions.''

"The way you've let your feelings influence what you think is best?" he challenged.

That was really the crux of her dilemma. She didn't know how much her feelings for Adam were influencing her judgment. But then she had so clearly misjudged him, surely her heart must be leading her in the right direction. She ran her hands through her hair. Her mind was going in circles.

"Did it ever occur to you," Adam said, broaching the problem that bothered him the most now, "that your absolute blind devotion to Verbena doesn't do either of you any good?"

"I think 'blind devotion' is more than a slight exaggeration, Adam," she said defensively. "You make me sound like a German Shepherd."

"You must read Verbena's rough drafts and manuscripts."

"Of course I—"

"Then why didn't you have the guts to tell her how bad the last book was? Think of all the humiliation you could have saved her if you had only had the courage to tell her it needed rewriting."

"How dare you imply that I—"

"Or were you afraid that you and she would argue? That she would be hurt or disappointed in you? Couldn't you even risk that possibility enough to help her?"

Leah went white with anger. "I told you that in confidence! About my—my family and how I—I—" She stammered to a halt, becoming too emotional to speak.

Adam relented. He softened his voice, but he couldn't be sorry he had brought it out into the open. "It's still in confidence, Leah. But you treat it like a guilty secret. Do you think your parents were angry with you when they died? Of course not. You and your sister had probably been through that same situation a hundred times. Hadn't you?"

"Yes, but—"

"It was just another day to them."

"I know that, but—"

"But what? You think Verbena will die if you do any-thing to upset her? Leah, it's no wonder you haven't been home for two years. It can't be money. Verbena would send you a ticket every single weekend if she thought you could come. But you know that as soon as you arrive you have to be patient, loving and supportive every minute of the day and take on a lot of responsibilities you don't want. She loves you. And she runs her life happily—if chaotically—when you're not here. Do you honestly think she would get irretrievably angry if you told her you just wanted to relax for a change? If you disagreed with her latest theories or told her her book needed more work? If you lost your temper with her for once?"

"Oh, Adam, it's not that easy," she said shakily, feeling raw and exposed.

"I know it's not, honey," he said tenderly. "We all have demons in our past that affect our lives. I still can't help re-senting the whole academic world—mostly because it didn't want me as badly as I wanted it."

"I feel so guilty," she admitted. "It's true. Every time I think of coming home, it just sounds so exhausting. But I love Verbena. I love coming home, only..."

Adam kissed her hand. "It's time to let go of your night-mares, Leah, just like you need to let go of your prejudices, if..."

"If what?" Her voice trembled.

"If we're going to be more than a summer fling."

Their eyes met and held. He had just voiced her greatest longing and most painful fear. She was confused, dis-tressed, emotionally exhausted.

"Everything is changing since I met you," she whis-pered.

"For me, too."

Tears started to slide down her cheeks. "I don't know what's right for me anymore."

"Leah." He stood and rounded the table. She shot out of her chair and flung herself against him. "I'm scared, too," he confessed.

"Please, just hold me. Right now, just hold me. I can't think anymore right now."

"I will, it's all right," he soothed.

"Please, Adam . . ."

"What, honey?"

"Make love to me. I need . . . you."

He swept her up into his arms and carried her out of the kitchen, leaving their unfinished dinner sitting on the table, a tempting target for the menagerie. Leah kissed and caressed him all the way up to his bedroom. When they tumbled across the crisp sheets, they stripped away their robes, and all their inhibitions.

The night held magic for Leah. Passion swept through her body like spiced wine, heady and overpowering. Adam offered gifts she had never dreamed of, and he asked for everything in return. He made love to her with honesty, frankness and commitment, weaving a spell around her that she knew would last long after the night had ended. Nothing in her life had prepared her for the burning, unashamed ecstasy they shared together in that sultry room.

When they lay quietly together at last, drained of all energy, they spoke softly about inconsequential things, enjoying their closeness, their discoveries, their pillow talk.

"So how did you get interested in history in the first place?" Leah asked drowsily, combing her fingers through the hair on his chest.

"It was a girl, of course."

"Of course," she said dryly.

"My senior year in high school, a new girl moved to town and became president of the history club. I fell in love at first sight. But she wasn't impressed by my football playing, or my fast driving, or my tight jeans. I was at a loss."

"I can just imagine."

"So I joined the history club, hoping to get her attention."

"And?"

"And she finally decided to go out with me. To make a long story short, I lost interest in the girl after a few weeks—she had no sense of humor, hated pizza and chewed gum incessantly—but I fell in love with the subject. The puzzles and mysteries; the stories that were too improbable for fiction but actually happened; the individual lives that shaped whole eras, nations and ideologies. Well, hell, I guess I don't have to sell *you*."

"No. I know exactly what you mean. Do you ever think about teaching someday? As well known as you are, you're bound to be asked eventually. Not all universities are as narrow-minded as Barrington was."

"'Narrow-minded'?" he repeated in amusement. "Listen to you, jumping to my defense again."

She remained silent.

"I don't know if I'll ever teach. I think I would like to. I think I could make the subject accessible to a lot of kids who might major in something else if someone like Melchior Browning got his hands on them first. But I'm also very busy—writing, researching, speaking, working as a consultant to films and television." Then he asked curiously, "Do you want to teach?"

"Yes. But then I was raised in the heart of established academia."

"You'll be a good teacher," he said with certainty. He added wryly, "All the kids will be terrified of you at first, then all the boys will fall in love with you and all the girls will come to you with their problems."

"What about my brilliant academic mind?" she asked dryly.

"That goes without saying. But you have a lot of fringe benefits that most professors don't." His hands emphasized his opinion.

Their voices grew softer as they slowly, contentedly, drifted off to sleep. They had temporarily forgotten the emotional turmoil of the evening, lulled and comforted as they were by the pleasure they found in merely being together.

Leah's subconscious, however, wouldn't let her evade the issues. She woke up in the middle of the night, disturbed by dreams that played out her worst fears: losing Verbena, losing Mordred, losing control and—worst of all now—losing Adam.

Adam rested peacefully beside her, cradling her in his arms and pinning her to the mattress with a muscular thigh. A vague sense of unease, a nagging feeling that she had forgotten something, crept over her as she stared at the ceiling.

Mordred! She hadn't been to see him since this morning. He must be starving by now! And frightened, bored, uncomfortable and thoroughly annoyed with her. She glanced warily at Adam's closed eyes. Despite his morning sluggishness, he had so far proved to be a very light sleeper. She wondered if she could slip away to visit Mordred and sneak back unnoticed.

Slowly, ever so gently, she started to ease herself out of Adam's arms. He grunted in his sleep and tightened his hold on her. She rolled her eyes nervously. She painstakingly slid one leg out from beneath the heavy weight of his. No reaction. She took a shallow breath and tried to free the other leg.

For five minutes she squirmed and wriggled as delicately as she could. Finally losing patience, she pulled herself away from the comforting, enticing warmth of his body and started to slide off the bed.

"What's wrong?" he asked faintly.

Her heart nearly stopped beating. "Nothing's wrong," she whispered.

"Where are you going?"

"Nowhere."

"Yes, you are."

She could tell by his voice that her answers were making him more alert rather than soothing him. Sighing in defeat, she slid back next to him and snuggled into his embrace. Mordred would just have to wait until morning.

Contrary to her expectations, Leah slept later than Adam the next morning. And the way he woke her up pushed all thoughts of Mordred out of her mind for quite a long time.

Adam might not be capable of intelligent conversation first thing in the morning, but that, Leah reflected, was really a very minor, insignificant flaw. Particularly since his physical prowess and emotional instincts were clearly at their best as the morning sun spread slowly across his bed.

While he was in the shower she found her chance for escape. She told Adam she would be changing in her room, and dashed down to the kitchen, where she prepared a great deal of food, not knowing when she would have another chance to slip away from Adam without making awkward explanations. She let the bread knife clatter to the floor when she thought she heard Adam's step behind her. To her relief, it was just Macbeth.

As she ran out the back door, she decided that she really must convince Mordred to turn himself in. Her nerves couldn't stand the strain of lying to Adam and keeping secrets from him. What's more, Mordred couldn't hide out forever.

Adam stuck his head into Leah's room to tell her he had finished in the bathroom if she wanted to use it. "Leah?" he said, puzzled when he saw no sign of her.

Through her open window he heard the hollow thud of the back porch door as it swung shut. He crossed the room and looked down into the yard, thinking he would call to her. As soon as he saw her, the words died on his lips.

She was carrying an enormous tray of food: sandwiches, soup, a pitcher of iced tea, part of their leftover pizza, several slices of pie. He frowned, wondering why on earth she had prepared all that food first thing in the morning.

Then he saw the candles as she passed directly under the window. Why did she need candles? Instead of placing her burdensome tray down by the hammock, she carried it off into the woods. A terrible feeling of uneasiness stole across him as he remembered thinking he had seen the flare of a match in the woods last night. It could have been the flicker of a candle, briefly glimpsed.

Wearing only his cutoffs and a tank top, he ran barefoot down the stairs, through the house and out the back door, determined to follow Leah and find out at last what she was hiding from him.

He ran across the lawn and followed Leah's path into the woods, slowing down so he wouldn't come upon her suddenly and give himself away. As he walked stealthily through the grass, he felt an uncomfortable prickly sensation, as if he were being watched.

He shook off the feeling after a moment. After all, he was the one doing the following. And his nerves were wound tight as a trap ready to spring.

Mordred fell on the food with glad little cries, devouring it voraciously and closing his eyes in ecstasy.

"I can't keep waiting for him to shower so I can sneak out here, Mordred," Leah was saying worriedly.

"Why can't you come at night, after he's gone to bed?" Mordred said between bites.

"I . . . He's a very light sleeper," she said weakly.

Mordred stared at her. "The room you're staying in is three rooms away from his room. How lightly can he sleep?"

Abandoning that argument, Leah tried another. "Some men showed up yesterday. They said they were Special Attachment, Security and Intelligence. Does that mean anything to you?"

"Bureaucratic double-talk."

"I think they've guessed that I know where you are, and they won't let up until I tell them. Mordred, please, for my sake, for your own sake—"

"Leah, I can't! Don't ask me! I'll never see daylight again."

"What could you have done that could be so bad? They'll slap you on the wrist, maybe fine you and then let you go."

"You can't seriously believe that?" he cried, getting hysterical again. "Didn't you read *The Bourne Identity*? You know what they did to *him* when he tried to give himself up!"

"I can't believe they'll do that to you. I'll stand by you, I promise, I won't let anything happen to you. But I . . ." Her voice started trembling and tears started to roll down her cheeks.

"Oh, Leah," he said, becoming emotional himself. He put down his pizza. "Please, don't cry. *Please*. You never cry. I can't stand this."

"Mordred," Leah said, pacing in front of him, "Verbena's off in London with a convalescent anthropologist. I'm looking after a neurotic ferret, a gigantic iguana, a foulmouthed mynah bird, three dogs, and cats that seem to be multiplying in number every day. I've alienated a professor I admired because I found out he's a hypocritical, unprincipled jerk. I've got Ralu, goddess of the underworld, chanting and burning incense daily in the house, in the vain hope that I can get the housekeeper to come back to work. I'm falling in love with a man who's turned my whole life upside down. I haven't gotten a lick of work done on my thesis, I'm being harassed by men in badly tailored suits and I'm hiding a fugitive in the backyard. Mordred, *I can't take any more*."

Verging on hysteria herself, she seized the front of his shirt and started shaking him.

"Leah, calm down," he squeaked. "We can discuss this!"

"Don't do this to me! Please!"

There were muffled voices coming from inside the tumbledown shed when Adam approached it. Suddenly he heard Leah's voice.

"Don't do this to me! Please!"

Motivated by primitive, urgent emotions, Adam made an inarticulate sound of fury—the male of the species protecting its mate—and threw himself bodily at the door.

The scene inside blurred before his enraged eyes. He saw Leah grappling with a dark-haired young man. They both turned panic-stricken faces toward him as he burst into the room.

The young man tightened his hold on Leah. Adam snarled and leaped forward, ready to kill the stranger for threatening her.

"No!" Leah screamed and threw herself in Adam's path.

They flew smack against each other and went tumbling to the floor with a heavy, spine-jarring thud. They rolled across the grimy surface and landed against the wall in a tangled heap of arms and legs.

The stranger sank into a far corner. He drew a trembling hand across his face and gulped sporadic breaths of air. "I'm never coming home again," he said. "It's far too traumatizing."

Winded, dazed and in not-inconsiderable pain, Adam raised his head and looked incredulously at the stranger. "Mordred?" he croaked.

"Yes!" Leah hissed breathlessly. "That's Mordred."

She painfully hauled herself to her feet. Her eyes rested on her cousin. "Are you okay?"

"Is *he* okay?" Adam demanded, wounded pride fueling his sense of outrage. "You just nearly broke *my* neck!"

"And you nearly scared him into cardiac arrest!" she snapped.

"What's he doing out here?" Adam demanded.

"Who the devil are you?" Mordred said.

"Adam Jordan."

"Adam Jordan?" Mordred paused for a moment. "Hey, I've heard of you! I've read two of your books. I loved *They Also Serve*. Say, is that true about prostitutes in the sixteenth century? I mean, the way they used to—"

"Mordred, this is hardly the time to swap lurid masculine tales," Leah said irritably.

"For once I agree with you," Adam said. "What the hell do you think you're doing hiding him out here?"

"Don't talk to me in that tone of voice," Leah said.

"Have you lost your mind?" Adam persisted. "And I thought perhaps I had been too hard on you last night! This time you've really carried things too far. How long were you planning to keep this a secret?"

"Now see here—" Mordred said.

"You keep out of this," Adam snapped.

"Don't talk to him that way!" Leah cried.

"He has evidently disrupted a major data systems company, possibly destroying years of valuable research, and you're hiding him from their security people." Adam looked at them both with disgust. "I don't know which one of you to throttle first!"

"Wait, wait," Leah interrupted. "Did you say a *data systems* company?"

"Yes." He looked at their blank faces. "The guys that were here yesterday," he prodded.

Leah still looked blank.

"Who did they say they worked for?" Mordred asked slowly.

"RMQE," Adam said.

"RMQE?" Mordred repeated. "*That's* who's chased me all the way across the country?" He turned accusingly on his cousin. "Why didn't you tell me?"

"Who are RMQE?" Leah said helplessly.

"Don't you ever read anything but your history books?" Mordred said in exasperation. "They're a major international company. Space-age technology, defense contracts, medical developments."

"What did you do to them?" Adam demanded.

"That's what we'd like to discuss," said a voice from the doorway.

Leah, Adam and Mordred all whirled around. Six tall men, all wearing dark suits and sober expressions, stood at the entrance to the shed. Two of them were armed.

Leah went white as a sheet. Mordred turned green. Adam shook his head in disbelief. "How, from an ordinary life in Cudahay, Wisconsin, did I ever reach this point?" he asked morosely.

"Who are they?" Leah whispered.

"The Untouchables?" Mordred croaked.

The man in the doorway actually cracked a smile. "No, sir. I'm Gibson. This here is Bryniarski. And the others are just here to back us up. You've been mighty hard to catch, Mr. McCargar." He spoke briefly into a walkie-talkie, telling his contact that he had found their suspect and was about to take him into custody.

"I don't suppose if I said, 'I'm sorry,' you'd let the whole matter drop?" Mordred asked hopefully.

Gibson shook his head. "No. We have quite a few things we'd like to ask you, Mr. McCargar. And your friends. I think we'd all better go back up to the house."

Adam, Mordred and Leah all went with their escorts. The despair in Mordred's eyes made Leah feel guilty. She had unwittingly led them straight to him.

The fury in Adam's eyes cut her much more deeply. Could he ever forgive her for getting him involved in this?

He was right. This time she really had carried family loyalty too far. She would have to change her ways before she made a mess of her life.

She glanced at Adam's tense expression and wondered painfully if it was already too late.

Eleven

At Gibson's request, they all went into the study and closed the door on the menagerie, who had greeted the newcomers with playful glee. Bryniarski obviously adored animals and forgot his responsibilities for a moment. Two of the men were terrified of the timid Questing Beast.

Gibson wanted to break up the party. He intended to separate Leah, Adam and Mordred, assigning two men to each of them to question them in separate rooms.

"Absolutely not," Adam said.

"I think you are hardly in a position to object," Gibson pointed out.

"They *are* the ones with weapons," Leah cautioned.

"All I've seen so far," Adam said, crossing his arms and leaning casually against the door frame in the study, "is a few RMQE identity cards. You aren't federal, state or local authorities. In fact, you're trespassing."

"Don't antagonize me, Mr. Jordan," Gibson warned.

"Oh, you know who I am?"

"You weren't hard to spot. In any event, Bryniarski has read all your books."

"Actually, Mr. Jordan," Bryniarski began hopefully, "maybe you could autograph one or two..." He trailed off as the rest of the group looked at him incredulously.

Picking up Adam's argument, Leah said, "In point of fact, Mr. Gibson, you are merely the employee of a large capitalist company no doubt controlled by semiliterate tyrants who take pride in terrorizing—"

"Leah, you're not helping," said Adam repressively. "What Miss McCargar is trying to say, gentlemen, is that we will gladly cooperate with you provided you behave within your legal limits."

"The only reason the FBI and the CIA and a host of other operatives aren't here," Gibson said testily, "is that we've managed to keep this quiet. We have not done this for Mr. McCargar's benefit, but for our own. You can imagine, I'm sure, how embarrassing it is that he managed to breach our most secure computer system not once, but several times."

"Why the hell did you do a dumb thing like that?" Adam snapped at Mordred.

"Idle curiosity," Mordred said defensively. "Besides, if that's an example of how they protect top-secret documents—"

"Did you honestly think they'd let you waltz in and out of their system without—"

"Adam, please," Leah interrupted.

"Thank God the FBI isn't after me," Mordred said reverently.

Adam's blue eyes went icy with rage. "And you came here to endanger your cousin, thinking the feds were after you?"

"He had nowhere else—" Leah began.

"And you!" Adam whirled on her. "I know you're protective of your family, but you must have lost your mind! If they *were* the FBI, and not just some clowns from an overfinanced computer company, do you know what they'd *do* to you for hiding him?''

"Hey!" said Gibson resentfully.

"I couldn't just throw him to the wolves, Adam!" Leah said, pleading with him to understand.

"And hiding him in the shed struck you as a reasonable alternative?" Adam demanded.

"It was temporary!"

"Until what?"

"I don't know!"

"Why," he said, running his hands through his hair and rumpling it even more, "why couldn't you trust me? Why couldn't you just tell me he had shown up and was in trouble?"

"What would you have done?" she demanded. "Make me turn him in against his will?"

"Well, for one thing, *I* know who RMQE are and could have told you it wasn't so serious."

"Oh," she said humbly. It *was* a stupid mistake.

"Or we could have thought of another way to help him. Why didn't you tell me?"

"I'm used to handling things by myself."

"Leah." He stepped forward and put his hands on her shoulders. "That's the whole point. You don't have to. You don't have to take every one of your family's problems and treat it as your own."

"This wasn't something Mordred could handle," she protested.

"Then you could have shared it with me. That's what I'm here for. Do you honestly want to spend the rest of your life handling everything by yourself? Do you think all I'm good for is making love and—" He stopped himself, suddenly aware that they were the center of attention. The other seven men in the room watched them with riveted fascination.

"Go on, Mr. Jordan," urged Bryniarski sentimentally. "Tell her you love her."

Leah, who had been held spellbound by the light in Adam's eyes and the warmth in his voice, suddenly snapped back to reality. She blushed till her face burned.

"Excuse me, everybody," said Mordred sourly, "but do you think we could focus on *my* crisis for just a moment?"

"That is why we're all here," Gibson reminded Bryniarski.

The phone rang. Gibson granted Leah permission to answer it, as if he had the right to stop her. She picked up the receiver while Adam and Gibson argued about what they should all do next.

Leah returned to the group moments later. "Adam..." she said weakly.

"Yes?" He glanced over and saw with concern that she looked even more upset.

"That was Verbena."

"Professor McCargar?" said Bryniarski. "Say, Mr. Jordan, is it true that you two are working on a book together?"

"How did you know that?" Adam asked, frowning. It wasn't that widely known.

Bryniarski looked a little sheepish.

"You *did* bug the phones, didn't you?" Leah gasped. "And you made cryptic, threatening calls. Talk about an amateur operation!"

"We never threatened you," Gibson said quickly.

"If you run your computer security the way you've run this investigation, no wonder my cousin broke your codes so easily!" Leah said scathingly.

"Leah, please don't antagonize the man," Mordred said.

"What did you want to tell me, Leah?" Adam asked wearily.

She met his eyes. "Verbena is in New York waiting for the next available seat on a flight to Ithaca."

"She's here?" Adam and Mordred said simultaneously.

"Grimly has been driving her crazy ever since the operation."

"That's not surprising," said Mordred.

"So she left London and came home. She'll fly in and take a taxi from the airport."

Adam lowered his head in thought. Finally he said, "Gibson, we need to get this sorted out before she gets here."

"Unease! Great distress!" cried a voice in the entrance hallway.

"What the devil is that?" exclaimed Gibson.

"That's Ralu," Leah said. "If you've been watching the house, you must know about her."

"We've only been watching it since this morning. You mentioned a Ralu on the phone, but we thought—"

Ralu swept into the room and breathed deeply a few times. She waved her arms so that her multicolored caftan frightened the mynah bird, who began cursing at her in Middle English.

Within moments, Gibson decided to remove Mordred for questioning.

"You can't do that!" Leah said hotly.

"Miss McCargar, I *can* call the FBI and tell them that your cousin has been waltzing in and out of files containing information about a top-secret defense contract for the U.S. government. Now the choice is yours. Will he come willingly to our offices with me, or should I make that call?"

"The choice is *mine*," said Mordred quickly, "and I see no reason to bother the FBI with all this piddling nonsense."

"Adam," Leah pleaded, turning to him for help.

"It's all right, honey, I'll go with him. You stay here and wait for Verbena."

"But I . . ." She took a deep breath and nodded. He took her hand in his and squeezed it gently. She clung to it for a moment, drawing from his strength. "Call me," she said at last.

"We have a lot to talk about," he said sternly.

Leah watched apprehensively as Mordred, Adam and the RMQE team left in two cars. Her whole body was trembling and tense. She was relieved that RMQE wanted to deal with Mordred quietly and didn't intend to kill him or lock him up. She was grateful to Adam for his support, his common sense, his quick thinking and his loyalty.

She loved him till her heart ached, loved him more than anyone or anything. The worst moment of her life, she realized, was not when she thought they might kill Mordred, but when she thought that Adam might not be able to forgive her for going so far out on the limb to protect her family. She needed him more than anyone else in her life, needed his love, comfort, support, protection, humor, perspective. And as soon as he came home, she would tell him so.

The day provided another miracle in Leah's life. Ralu came downstairs to tell her that she had finally succeeded in escorting their uninvited guest across the great void. Jenny Harper would be in the next morning to start cleaning the house.

"It really needs it, too," Ralu added fastidiously before she swept out the door.

Since the day had already held so many adventures, Leah was astonished to look at the clock and find it was barely lunchtime. She fixed a huge lunch, just to give herself something to do, then stared at it for twenty minutes before giving it all to the menagerie. She couldn't eat a bite.

Nervous energy enabled her to do the necessary chores in under two hours. Still no word from Adam or Verbena. She wandered aimlessly, paced, shredded Kleenex. Finally she decided she would have to find something to concentrate on or she'd go crazy.

She knew she'd never get any valuable work done on her thesis today, although the source Adam had recommended to her provided some of the information she was looking for. She hated television and didn't feel like telephoning anyone. She went to a book-lined room and looked for something to read.

They Also Serve by Adam Jordan caught her eye instantly. It was a well-worn copy, as if Verbena had read it more than once. Her mind slowed down and stopped running in frantic circles.

How many times had Adam pointed out that she was judging him unfairly? She had always considered this sort of pop history a betrayal of the scholarly principles with which she had been raised. But knowing Adam as she did now, loving him loyally, she couldn't believe he would produce work she couldn't respect. She felt just a brief flash of fear as she sat down and opened the book. How would she face him if she didn't like it? She brushed the thought aside. She would learn to live with that. She would learn not to mind, because she loved him.

They Also Serve was a factual, fascinating, well-researched, well-written, witty and compassionate account of working women in the Middle Ages. There were precious few ways a woman could support herself in Medieval Europe. The book examined women in those life-styles, as well as women who were bound to men by filial or marital ties but nevertheless contributed skills, labor or land to the economy and the fabric of society.

She was deeply engrossed in her reading when she heard a voice from the doorway. "Why don't you turn on a light?"

She dropped the book and jumped out of her chair. "Adam! You scared the life out of me!"

"Leah, it's nearly eight o'clock, how can you even see what you're reading?" he chided, switching on a lamp. He picked up the book and then stopped in his tracks. His questioning gaze sought her eyes.

"I...needed something to keep my mind off of... Where's Mordred?"

"Gibson will bring him back later," Adam assured her.

"You left him there alone?"

"Don't worry. Everything is all right."

"What happened?"

"Well, Mordred spent about two hours showing them how easily he had violated their security. Then he spent another four hours showing them various ideas he has about how they could improve their system. Then . . . I got a little lost after that, but the upshot of it is, they've offered him a job."

"What?" She was astounded.

"It was either that or turn him over to the FBI. He's evidently seen a lot of top-secret information. They can't let him back out on the streets unless they're assured he's loyal to them. Anyhow, they decided he was a genius, and it was safer to have him in their camp than in someone else's." Adam shook his head. "Between Mordred and Verbena, I guess I should be grateful that you turned out fairly normal."

Their eyes met.

"Ralu's gone for good. Jenny Harper will be here tomorrow," Leah said inanely.

"Well, that's a relief."

"So we really have nothing bad to tell Verbena."

"Yes, we do, Leah." His gaze was steady. "We have to tell her about me."

"I'll make her understand, Adam."

His brows rose. "Understand what?"

"That you should have gotten your degree. That she shouldn't lose respect for you just because you don't have a few extra letters after your name."

"Is that really what you think?" His voice was husky with emotion.

Leah nodded. "And if she doesn't agree with me . . . that's tough. I'll stand by you."

He smiled softly. "It's okay, Leah. I'll handle her. I don't want you to fend for me. I just wanted you to want to."

"Oh, Adam, I do." She sighed.

He drew her into his arms. "Bryniarski already said it for me, but I'll say it anyhow. I love you, Leah."

Their lips met with sweet ardor. They kissed again, and then smiled into each other's eyes. "I love you, too," Leah whispered. "And I'll tell her the truth. She needs you."

"She does?"

"You're a *wonderful* writer, Adam." She picked up *They Also Serve*. "This is a great book. It's the only thing that could have taken my mind off of everything today." She told him what she thought of it, pointing out her favorite parts and exclaiming on all the details she hadn't known. When he started to look a little smug, she added critically, "Of course, you generalize a little too much here and there, and I really don't agree with your theory about—"

He laughed with delight. "Leah, we can talk about this later. For now, I'm just relieved to know you don't think you'll be living with an intellectual leper."

"Living with?"

"You are going to marry me, aren't you?" he said silkily, pulling her back into his arms.

"As long as you don't think you'll be living with an academic snob," she said seriously.

"No," he said, "I don't. Not anymore. And I promise I'll even be nice to all your colleagues."

"They'd just better be nice to you," she said fiercely.

He hugged her. "They will, if a respected professor like you will be my wife."

At that point the menagerie went wild. Barking, meowing and mewling, half a dozen animals headed toward the front door.

"Verbena must be home," said Adam wryly.

Moments later they heard Verbena's voice in the hallway, exclaiming with delight as she greeted each of her beloved pets. She greeted them last when they came out of the study.

"Grimly's going back to his Amazonian jungle next week," Verbena said. "The doctors told him he was crazy, but you know how little store he puts in anyone else's opinion."

"That reminds me," Leah exclaimed as they all sat down in the kitchen. "Mordred has come home, after all."

"He has?" Verbena's whole face lit up. "Where is he?"

Adam cleared his throat. "With friends. He'll be here later."

They listened to Verbena for a half hour as she recounted her adventures in London, told Adam excitedly about some new sources she had uncovered and handed Leah the letters from the British Museum's library that Adam had recommended to her.

"So what's been happening here?" Verbena asked at last.

Adam and Leah exchanged a glance.

"Not much," said Leah.

"Dull as dishwater," said Adam.

"Just work and study," said Leah.

"Same old routine," said Adam.

"I knew you would both handle everything fine," said Verbena placidly.

"Verbena," said Adam with determination in his voice. "There's something I have to tell you."

"There's something *we* have to tell you, Auntie."

"Leah, please, this is my problem, I can handle it," said Adam patiently.

"I was the one who insisted you tell her in the first place," Leah argued.

"I told you I meant to tell her anyhow," he said.

"Tell me what?" said Verbena.

"Verbena, I never—"

"Adam was unfairly—" Leah interrupted.

"Leah, I'm an adult. Will you let me handle this?" he said in exasperation.

"I just thought—"

"Isn't this exactly the sort of thing that got us into so much trouble today?" he challenged.

Leah lowered her eyes. She nodded. "I'm sorry. It's just a hard habit to break." She shrugged. "I grew up believing certain things, and I need time to... adjust."

"Of course you do, but this is really my—"

"Would one of you mind telling me what you're talking about?"

Adam took a deep breath. "Verbena, before we go any further, you should know that I never got my Ph.D. at Barrington."

"I know that, Adam."

Leah and Adam both stared at her in shocked silence.

"Well, of course, I know it," Verbena said patiently. "I helped you get into Barrington. I kept an eye on your career. I knew they were trying to kick you out when you quit."

"You *knew*?" Leah repeated incredulously. "And yet you still—"

"I have avoided discussing this with you, Leah, because I love you," said Verbena. "I couldn't love you more if you were my own daughter. I didn't want to say harsh words to you. I still don't, but it seems I must. I know, as the scholar who raised you, that I am to blame, but, Leah, dear, you're something of a snob."

"I . . ." Leah was dumbfounded.

"The degrees do not make the man, Leah. Nor does a book need to be inaccessible in order to be scholarly. Adam is a fine young historian who had been mistreated by the academic community."

After a profound silence, Adam spread his hands helplessly and said, "If you knew, why didn't you say something?"

"I thought it might embarrass you," Verbena said. "I had assumed that you and Melchior must have buried your differences four years ago when he gave you that honorary degree. I couldn't understand why you were still so hostile to each other. And then, when he purposely told that dreadful story at lunch, I realized how much he and other unimaginative scholars resent you. And how much you must resent the way they look down on your work, even when it's better than theirs."

Adam chuckled. "You're always full of surprises, Verbena."

"I'm ashamed to admit that for years I shared Melchior's narrow-minded views about books, theories and qualifications. And I think it's a wonder that you have overcome a very natural resentment to the established academic community—a community that already recognizes you more than you realize."

"I've had my share of resentment," Adam admitted, "but you and Leah are changing all that. I can't keep on detesting professors if I'm working with one and married to another."

It was Verbena's turn to look stunned. "You're marrying him?" she said to Leah.

Leah nodded.

"I'm... quite overcome." After a moment, Verbena smiled brilliantly. "I'm so pleased you two have surmounted your petty differences. What a wonderful wedding we'll have!"

"Wedding?" Adam repeated.

"Wedding?" Leah said nervously.

"Yes. And I'll plan everything!"

Leah's stomach starting churning. "Oh, no, Auntie, I don't think there's time. I have to go back to California at the end of summer...."

"Right. And I'm going with her, as soon as I sublet my place in Boston," Adam added quickly. He looked desperately at Leah. The thought of a wedding planned by Verbena was more than even his nerves could handle.

"Then we must have it this summer!" exclaimed Verbena. "Who knows when we'll all be here together again, you, Mordred and I. We can't let this opportunity pass!"

"Really, Auntie, we were thinking of just a quiet civil service...."

"No fuss, no mess—" Adam added.

"Oh, no, you can't! This is the only wedding I'll ever get to plan. We'll have it right here, in the backyard." She frowned. "Of course, we'll have to find a justice of the peace who's not afraid of animals."

Adam groaned as he pictured his wedding day fraught by the terrors of Verbena's household: a Shih Tzu chewing on Leah's dress; a mynah bird swearing at his mother and father; a ferret cradled in the matron of honor's arms; an iguana lurking around the refreshments table.

"Verbena, no," he said sternly. Leah glanced at him in anguish. "Leah, someone around here has to start putting their foot down."

Verbena's eyes filled with tears. She made a brave little effort to speak, then swallowed hard. "Very well, Adam," she said at last. "If you don't want...to be married here...in the house you met Leah in...where we've all spent so many happy hours..."

Adam felt his resolve weakening.

Leah rolled her eyes. "Go on, Adam, show me how tough you are," she whispered slyly.

"This is what you've been up against all these years," he murmured back, the full weight of his situation starting to penetrate.

"You'll all go back to California soon...and I'll be here alone...without even memories of the wedding...."

Adam looked desperately to Leah for help. She smiled maliciously.

He sighed deeply. "All right, Verbena. We'll do it."

"Oh, thank you, Adam!" Verbena's sunny smile filled the room. She spent the next ten minutes waxing poetic about how wonderful it would all be. She went upstairs to unpack at last, muttering about how beautiful the menagerie might look in bows of matching colors.

Leah grinned and slid onto Adam's lap. "That was a good first round, Adam, but you're clearly still an amateur."

He groaned and buried his face in her hair.

"And to think," she chided, "that you've criticized me for not being able to say no to her. You do realize, don't you, that in addition to writing and researching, you and I are going to get stuck with planning the wedding that she wants us to have?''

"I know," he said bleakly. "It was just the way she looked . . . the way she said . . ." He pulled away to look into her face. "Okay. I admit it. I'm sorry I criticized you so much."

Leah laughed at his despairing expression. "And she had barely turned the screws."

"I'm going to co-write the rest of this book long-distance," he said firmly.

"So you don't relish the thought of me coming back to Ithaca to teach eventually, if I get a job offer?" she teased.

He looked a little pale under his golden tan. "Maybe we could stay in California." Then a new thought occurred to him. "No, RMQE told Mordred they'd be sending him back there. Maybe you could find a job sort of halfway between the two. It would at least give us a fighting chance for a normal life." He buried his face in her hair again. "A normal life? Who am I kidding?"

She tilted his chin up and kissed him. "I love you," she whispered.

His hands slipped under her blouse. "I was hoping we could get married this week," he murmured, "so we could sleep in the same bed without embarrassing her."

"I could creep into your room after everyone's gone to bed." Leah's hands slid down his chest.

He kissed her chin, her jaw, her neck, and then pressed her palm to his cheek. "Well, I'm certainly not going to sneak into *your* bed. Everyone in the house would hear the sloshing."

"Hmm," she sighed as his hands moved caressingly over her back. "And then I could sneak back out in the morning. Of course, the way *you* are in the mornings, you probably won't even remember I've been there."

"Oh, I'll remember all right. I'm pretty used to you already."

Their kisses grew more passionate, their hands more demanding, their needs more urgent Their breath was harsh and rapid when they pulled apart again.

"Your room, in about a half hour?" Leah suggested breathlessly.

"It's a date." He stopped her when she tried to slide off his lap. "Oh, how long before we can get married?"

"Now that you've agreed to Verbena's plans," she said, arching her brows critically, "as long as it takes to plan the wedding."

"Let's start on it full-time tomorrow. With luck, we could be married before Verbena figures out we're already enjoying our conjugal couch."

"Okay." She smiled and kissed him again. "Till then, it'll be our secret."

She slipped out of the room, pleased to have had the last word with him for a change.

* * * * *

SILHOUETTE Desire™

COMING NEXT MONTH

#565 TIME ENOUGH FOR LOVE—Carole Buck
Career blazers Doug and Amy Hilliard were *just too busy*...until they traded the big city winds for the cool country breezes and discovered the heat of their rekindled passion.

#566 BABE IN THE WOODS—Jackie Merritt
When city-woman Eden Harcourt got stranded in a mountain cabin with Devlin Stryker, she found him infuriating—infuriatingly *sexy*! This cowboy was trouble from the word go!

#567 TAKE THE RISK—Susan Meier
Traditional Caitlin Petrunak wasn't ready to take chances with a maverick like Michael Flannery. Could this handsome charmer convince Caitlin to break out of her shell and risk all for love?

#568 MIXED MESSAGES—Linda Lael Miller
Famous journalist Mark Holbrook thought love and marriage were yesterday's news. But newcomer Carly Barnett knew better—and together they made sizzling headlines of their own!

#569 WRONG ADDRESS, RIGHT PLACE—Lass Small
Linda Parsons hated lies, and Mitch Roads had told her a whopper. Could this rugged oilman argue his way out of the predicament...or should he let love do all the talking?

#570 KISS ME KATE—Helen Myers
May's *Man of the Month* Giles Channing thought Southern belle Kate Beaumont was just another spoiled brat. But beneath her unmanageable exterior was a loving woman waiting to be tamed.

AVAILABLE NOW:

SILHOUETTE DESIRE™
presents
AUNT EUGENIA'S TREASURES
by CELESTE HAMILTON

Liz, Cassandra and Maggie are the honored recipients of Aunt Eugenia's heirloom jewels...but Eugenia knows the real prizes are the young women themselves. Read about Aunt Eugenia's quest to find them everlasting love. Each book shines on its own, but together, they're priceless!

Available in December:
THE DIAMOND'S SPARKLE (SD #537)

Altruistic Liz Patterson wants nothing to do with Nathan Hollister, but as the fast-lane PR man tells Liz, love is something he's willing to take *very* slowly.

Available in February:
RUBY FIRE (SD #549)

Impulsive Cassandra Martin returns from her travels... ready to rekindle the flame with the man she never forgot, Daniel O'Grady.

Available in April:
THE HIDDEN PEARL (SD #561)

Cautious Maggie O'Grady comes out of her shell...and glows in the precious warmth of love when brazen Jonah Pendleton moves in next door.

SD-AET-1R

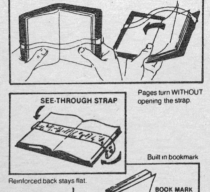

Just when you thought all the good men had gotten away, along comes ...

SILHOUETTE®

Desire™

MAN OF THE MONTH 1990

Twelve magnificent stories by twelve of your favorite authors.

In January, FIRE AND RAIN by Elizabeth Lowell
In February, A LOVING SPIRIT by Annette Broadrick
In March, RULE BREAKER by Barbara Boswell
In April, SCANDAL'S CHILD by Ann Major
In May, KISS ME KATE by Helen R. Myers
In June, SHOWDOWN by Nancy Martin
In July, HOTSHOT by Kathleen Korbel
In August, TWICE IN A BLUE MOON by Dixie Browning
In September, THE LONER by Lass Small
In October, SLOW DANCE by Jennifer Greene
In November, HUNTER by Diana Palmer
In December, HANDSOME DEVIL by Joan Hohl

Every man is someone you'll want to get to know ... and love. So get out there and find your man!